MARSHA MARTINEZ

MEETS THE STARS

Also by Jenny Oldfield:

Harmony Harris Cuts Loose

Series by Jenny Oldfield,
available from Hodder Children's Books:

Definitely Daisy
Totally Tom
My Little Life
The Wilde Family
Home Farm Twins
Horses of Half-Moon Ranch

MARSHA MARTINEZ

MEETS THE STARS

JENNY OLDFIELD

Hodder
Children's
Books

a division of Hodder Headline Limited

The king soon married another wife, who was very beautiful, but so proud that she could not bear to think that anyone could surpass her. She had a magical looking glass, to which she used to go and gaze upon herself in it, and say,

'Tell me, glass, tell me true!
Of all the ladies in the land,
Who is the fairest? Tell me who?'

And the glass answered,

'Thou, queen, art fairest in the land.'

But Snow-drop grew more and more beautiful; and when she was seven years old, she was bright as the day, and fairer than the queen herself. Then the glass one day answered the queen, when she went to consult it as usual,

'Thou, queen, may'st fair and beauteous be,
But Snow-drop is lovelier far than thee!'

When she heard this, she turned pale with rage and envy; and called to one of her servants and said, 'Take Snow-drop away into the wide wood, that I may never see her more.'

From Snow-drop, in German Popular Stories, collected by M. M. Grimm, 1823

One

Zadie thought she was doing me a favour when she snapped me with her brand-new Fuji Finepix A403 digital camera.

'Marsha might not look great in the flesh,' she told Dad, 'but the camera loves her!' Zadie showed everyone my mugshot.

Long, jet-black hair, pale skin, big suspicious eyes. Skinny-bilinky.

'Mirror, mirror, on the wall ...' Zadie chanted. 'I'm gonna enter her for "Face of the Year"!'

'Over my dead body,' I grunted. I'd only agreed to have my picture taken because she wanted to try out her Fuji.

Zadie's just started a photography course. She'd been pointing the lens aimlessly round the kitchen, and had decided I was a smidgeon more interesting than a box of cornflakes.

'Look this way!' she'd said. 'C'mon, Marsh, don't be a pain!' *Click-click.*

She'd shown me the pose on the tiny screen. *Beep-beep-bleep.* Then she'd given everyone in the room a glimpse – Dad, Sharon, Rochelle and Scott. Sharon's married to Dad, she's my stepmother. I'm not saying this is a bad thing, but it takes some getting used to.

'Doesn't she look cool?' Zadie had crowed.

They'd glanced at me over their toast and cereal. Scott had grunted, Rochelle had laughed. Sharon did at least tell her off for that.

'I never had my Marshmallow down as supermodel material,' Dad admitted.

Ho-ho, Dad!

He calls me 'my Marshmallow', which gets up Sharon's nose.

'Yeah, but the camera can make such a difference,' Zadie explained. 'Even the Kate Mosses of this world look bog ordinary when you see them in the street. It all depends on the angle, the lighting, capturing the right moment.' She dashed off to download the pic into the computer and print it off. 'Take a look at this!' she cried, slapping me down in full colour on the table.

I stared back at myself with my stroppy expression.

'I'm gonna enter it!' Zadie proclaimed. She'd read about the competition in my mag, and fancied she could take the winning shot.

Like I say, I'm sure she meant well. But she never asked my opinion – she just went ahead and did it. That's Zadie for you.

And me. I could've said something to stop her, but I never did. You'll have to get used to the fact that I'm the type that doesn't make a big thing out of things, and can never explain what I mean, even when I try. My words come out clumsy, like they did in that last sentence I wrote. So I keep quiet.

Sharon calls it sulking.

'Lay off, Shaz, she's only a kid,' Dad says.

Which drives her mad.

I came with Dad as part of the deal when Sharon married him. Sharon already had Zadie, Rochelle and Scott. There's photos of Zadie, Roche and me as bridesmaids. We're in pink silk, carrying starburst lilies. I'm wearing my stroppy look big-time.

Now Dad and Sharon have baby Florence between them, which is a good and a bad thing. Good because I like baby Flo and because it keeps Sharon off my back. Bad 'cos Dad doesn't give me much of a look-in either.

'What happens if you win?' Lisa asked.

Stef nearly wet her knickers. 'Hey, this is Marsh we're talking about!'

'Yeah, well she hasn't exactly got two heads, has she?'

'But Marsh!' Stef giggled.

jealous (say *jellus*) *adjective*
resentful or suspicious of a rival or another's
success, advantage etc.
[Greek *zelos* zeal]

By the way, I look words up. I like to know
about them. They come out wrong when I'm
talking, but at least *I* know what I mean.

Stef's a mate. I've known her since Year 3
in junior school. Weird thing – we were born
on the same day. We're both Leos. She fits
her star sign, whereas I don't.

I met Lisa a year ago, when we both
started at Granby. She's Virgo, a
perfectionist.

'What happens if Zadie's picture gets you
through to the next round?' she asked.

I shrugged. It was morning break and we
were stalking a couple of Scott's mates down
B corridor.

'Naff off, Marsha!' Scott snarled.

'Aah, back off, Scottie!' Ollie Sayer cut in.
'They're only little!'

Stef played along. 'Yeah, we're only ickle
Year 8s! Be nice to us!' Year 8 going on 18.

Stef's already into make-up and microskirts.

Enrique grinned at me. 'Keep your mate under control, Marsh.'

'I'll try,' I promised. I fancy Enrique, so I went tongue-tied and blushed bright red.

Luckily the lesson bell went and we split from the boys.

'If she wins, she gets to go to Leeds for a try-out with some major modelling agencies,' Lisa reported. 'I read it in *Dreamtime*. They dress her in designer gear and she struts her stuff on the catwalk. Cool!'

Stef frowned. 'When's the final entry date?'

'Too late. The competition's already closed,' Lisa told her.

The frown deepened and Stef stomped off to maths. She didn't save Lisa and me a seat. That's what I really call sulking.

resent (say *re-zent*) *verb*
to feel an indignant or angry dislike for
[RE + Latin *sentire* to feel]

'I won't win,' I told Lisa. 'I mean, look at me.'

And that wasn't me being fake. I look in a mirror and see big mouth. Big, *big* mouth. I'm all mouth, practically. And my ears aren't great either.

'No, I won't win. No chance.'

'Scott, take your feet off the table and move those magazines. Rochelle, run the baby's bath while I finish feeding her.' Sharon dishes out the orders and ignores me. Telling people what to do is her way of showing she cares. I carry on watching *Neighbours*.

Scott's feet stay where they are. He flicks to Sky for the footie.

'Hey, I was watching that!' I protest. Waste of breath.

'How's my little Flo-Jo!' Dad breezes in from a day on the road selling floor tiles. He scoops the baby out of her highchair and cuddles her on his knee.

'It's time for her bath,' Sharon says, whisking her away.

Rochelle is painting her plastic nails. She's one year older than Scott and three years older than me. She's hardly ever in. Dad and

Sharon argue over how much she's allowed to go out instead of doing her homework. Rochelle plans to stick with her Saturday job at the florist's when she leaves school and make it full time. Later, she's gonna find a premier division footballer and marry him.

'Why the chuffing-heck do I need GCSEs?' is her way of looking at it.

'You need to think further ahead,' Sharon tells her, but without meaning it. Sharon just left school and had babies. She made a career of it.

It's Dad who puts on the pressure. Like, 'You need qualifications to get your employers to respect you.'

Then there's a row and Roche yells that he's not her real dad and he can't tell her what to do. She storms out. That's how she handles it – by rowing and legging it.

But right now she's painting her nails and having a go at me.

'Shift yourself, Marsha. I can't see the telly.'

'It's only footie,' I mutter. I still want to know what happened in *Neighbours*.

'You're in my way!' she moans.

Which makes a change from being see-through, which is how she treats me most of the time. Marsha the Invisible Girl.

Dad shrugs and wanders off before he gets dragged in. *Thanks, Dad*.

'Hey, Dummy, did you hear what I said? Are you gonna shift, or what?'

Am I? What happens if I just sit here? I mean, Roche's nail polish is still wet, so she's not gonna smack me. But she can be nasty. Underneath the total babe outer shell is a control freak. Believe me, I know.

So I decide to move. I'm on my way up to my room when the front door opens and Zadie breezes in.

'Hiya!' she calls. She flings her bag on the floor and roots around on the hall table for a letter from her college. 'Oh no, I'm two weeks into term and my loan still hasn't arrived,' she groans. Then she finds an envelope tucked behind the fruit bowl and rips it open. 'This is for you, Marsha. It's from *Dreamtime!*'

I'm on the landing outside my room, but I

stop dead. It's two weeks since Zadie sent in my photograph, and I've been getting lousy stuff from Stef every day about it. Like, 'Have you heard yet?' and 'I bet you've had a letter saying you didn't make it, and you're just not telling us!'

This is it, then. The thing that says, '*Thank you for entering our competition, but it turns out you have a face like a car wreck, and no way could you qualify for the next round.*'

'I'm gobsmacked she even bothered to enter,' I overheard Stef telling Lisa the other day. She backtracked when she saw I was there, saying I mustn't take it the wrong way – it's just that models had to be fantastically drop-dead gorgeous to make it, even in a small way, and hey, we had to get real – none of us was that perfect!

I wasn't arguing with that, and I was waiting for the verdict with a sinking feeling, when Zadie gave a little yelp.

I felt my heart skip and flutter.

'Jeee-zus, I knew that was a great picture!' Zadie grinned. She waved the letter at me, then raced upstairs two at a time. Grabbing my arm, she dragged me into the bathroom, where Sharon was pouring perfumed water over Florence's chubby chest.

'Mum, guess what!' Zadie cried.

Sharon paused and glanced over her shoulder. When she saw me she turned back to the baby. 'What?' she mumbled.

'Marsha got through!'

Two

amaze *verb*
to surprise or astonish
astonish *verb*
to surprise greatly
surprise (say *sir-prize*) *noun*
something sudden or unexpected

Put it another way – I was gobsmacked.

We all were.

'Let me read that,' Rochelle said, then snatched the letter out of Zadie's hand. ' "Wanna be a top model and appear on the front cover of *Dreamtime*?" ' she read out loud. ' "You, Marsha Martinez, have star quality! Along with nine other glam girlies from the north who entered our competition, you're invited to a fantastic fashion shoot at a posh Leeds hotel." Puh-lease!'

I felt myself cringe. Glam girly was what I was not. You need to understand – I'm dead shy and hate people looking at me. If I can merge into the background, I'm happy.

'Are they serious?' Sharon asked, nearly drowning poor Florence.

Glug-glug. The baby made like a fish.

'It's not April the first, is it?' Roche retorted nastily, while Zadie grabbed the letter back.

' "Pinch yourself and tell yourself you're not dreaming",' she read on. ' "On October 30th you, Marsha, will meet top scouts from the big model agencies, plus *Dreamtime*'s very own fashion editor, Stacey Nicholls."

' "Expert make-up artists, hair stylists and dressers will be on hand to transform your Look. Then you'll strut your stuff on the catwalk while seriously successful fashion photographer, Domenico Lane, takes your pic."

'Domenico Lane!' Zadie's voice rose to a

squeak at the photographer's name. She repeated it twice. 'He's the hottest guy in his field! Wow, this is so cool!'

You might see this as a dream come true. A lot of people would.

And I'd be lying if I said part of me wasn't dead excited. Yeah, I'd had those secret moments of sitting on the top deck of the bus, just minding my own business and fantasizing about being spotted by a talent scout who would whisk me off into a studio and turn me into a mega successful fashion model. Or pop idol. Or Hollywood star.

Who, me?

Yeah, you. You have that natural, innocent look they're all going for. Not pretty-pretty. Maybe more ugly-pretty actually. But that's what the magazine editors and top Paris designers want right now.

So I was laughing inside, and going 'Hey, this is really happening!', but I was also probably about eighty per cent dreading it.

October 30th was this coming Monday.

Today was Friday. That left a whole weekend for my nerves to get torn to shreds.

'Marsha, get changed out of your school things and put them in the laundry basket,' Sharon snapped, turning her back and fishing in the froth for Flo's plastic frog. 'And don't let this competition go to your head.'

'Yeah,' Rochelle agreed. 'No way do I wanna listen to you showing off in front of your mates!'

envy (say *en-vee*) *noun*
a feeling of discontent aroused by seeing another's good fortune, superiority etc., usually accompanied by a desire to possess the advantages of the other person

'At least I've *got* mates,' I muttered. Then made a quick exit.

Monday afternoon, at the Riverside. Lights, camera, action! I shuddered at the thought.

'I'll come with you,' Zadie offered. 'I'll take the day off from lectures.'

'Thanks.'

'No problem.' Meaning, she would get to meet the great Domenico and show him her portfolio, or whatever it's called. Zadie's the ambitious one in our family – not that I didn't appreciate her taking the time off to be there.

'I can't go through with it,' I told Lisa when I met her and Stef outside Topshop next morning. 'Honest, I'd rather die!'

'God, Marsh, you don't half exaggerate!' Stef sighed.

So this is another side of me you have to get used to. I do go OTT sometimes.

'OK, then – maybe not die,' I admitted. 'Walk on hot coals, then. Yeah, I'd rather blister my feet to billyo. How would you like to parade in front of a bunch of people you don't know, with a zillion camera bulbs flashing?'

'Cool!' Stef assured me, gliding down the escalator.

'And have them pulling you to pieces inch by inch, saying your ears are way too big and what a laugh to think you could ever make it as a model!' We were inside the shop, surrounded by giant pics of kids in Topshop gear, all glitzy and glam for a disco.

'Give me half a chance!' Stef said, rummaging through the halter-necks.

'Don't do it if you don't want to,' Lisa advised. 'But I think you'd be a fool if you back out.'

'You're saying I have to go?'

She gave me a full-on stare over the row of padded jackets. 'Marsha, don't go on about it,' she pleaded. 'Either do it, or not. I just don't want the earache, that's all.'

Lisa's going through a bad time – her big brother's got problems and he's due in court for shoplifting. I could see how I might be getting on people's nerves wittering on about stupid stuff like Face of the Year, so I shut up.

'Duh-dah! What d'you think?' Stef asked, emerging from the changing room in an orange Lycra strapless top.

'Ouch!' Zadie was plucking my eyebrows and the tweezers had slipped.

'Wimp!' *Tweeze-tweeze*. 'D'you wanna win this contest, or not?'

'No. Yeah. I dunno. What am I gonna wear?' I whinged. 'I can't turn up in my school uniform, can I?'

Yeah, by now even *you're* getting sick of me moaning. I'm sorry. I'll try not to.

Pluck-pluck. She was giving me eyebrows that arched up like seagulls' wings, instead of ones that looked like furry hamsters squatting over my eyes.

'Borrow something from Rochelle.'

That was like saying send a little fluffy rabbit in with a Rottweiler.

'What? Why not? You're the same dress size, aren't you?'

Er – Rochelle – I need something to wear to the Riverside. How about lending me your Diesel jeans?

'Ouch!' I felt the tears come to my eyes.

Get lost, you little runt! Wear your own manky jeans!

Right from the start, Rochelle had been dead set on hating me.

I remember the first time we met, five

years ago. Cue violins and moonlight – *not!*

Sharon Hoddle visited Dad and me at Forest Lane. She piled out of the car with Scott and Rochelle, rang the doorbell and invited herself in for a cuppa. 'You've sold me two grand's worth of floor tiles,' she quipped. 'I was just passing, and I thought the least you could do is give us a cup of tea!'

Dad is a sucker for the jokey, up-front stuff from women. He put the kettle on, and it seems in my head that after this Sharon and her kids never went home.

Dad and she fell madly, deeply, truly in lurve.

Three months later the whole Hoddle brood moved in with us on Forest Lane, then we got this bigger house on Wentworth Road, perfectly tiled throughout. My dad sells them for a living, and flies to Spain to source them. He's half-Spanish, by the way.

Anyhow, that first time with the cuppa, Scott strolls in and parks himself in front of the telly. Rochelle hangs back with a scowl on her face. She sees seven-year-old me, and if looks could kill I'd be dead meat. I mean it.

Nothing's changed in the five years since then. She hates me and I hate her. Scott's still watching the telly. No kidding.

Roche is the one people notice. 'Legs up to her armpits,' Sharon says proudly. 'She gets those from her dad.'

Plus light brown hair which she wears short, spiky and highlighted. Big, pale grey eyes and dark lashes. Spends hours getting ready to go out, falls into a foul mood and takes it out on me if she can't find the hair straighteners, but she can always turn on the charm when she wants.

'Roche, Marsha can borrow stuff from you for Monday, can't she?' Zadie called downstairs while my hamster eyebrows vanished and the seagull soared over my smarting eyes.

'Get lost!' Roche replied.

'She says yes,' Zadie grinned. 'Listen, kid, you're gonna sail through this regional heat and get yourself down to London for the final if it's the last thing I do!'

Zadie – twenty years old. Dossed around for a bit after her 'A' levels. Has a boyfriend called Jude. First year photography student, like I said.

Talks big. Thinks big. Does what she has to do to get what she wants.

Sounds lousy, but to be honest, you know where you are with Zadie, and I get on better with her than I do with Rochelle. Not hard, I admit.

I'm the odd one out in the Hoddle huddle. Sharon, Zadie, Scott and Rochelle Hoddle versus Tony and Marsha Martinez. Hoddle United versus Martinez City. Only I'm not sure which team Dad's playing for any more.

Back to Zadie.

'Meet me at half-twelve outside the Riverside,' she tells me on Monday morning as I set off for school clutching my note.

'*Dear Mr Adams, Please excuse Marsha from*

lessons this afternoon, as she has to go to the Face of the Year contest in Leeds. Yours sincerely, David Martinez.'

I'm carrying an extra bag with my gear for the fashion shoot – Roche's jeans and trainers, Zadie's tight-fitting leather jacket. Make-up bag, brush.

'Good luck, Marshmallow,' Dad called as he left the house at seven-thirty. 'Look after her, Zadie,' he added.

I'm feeling sick with nerves.

'There are two doors into the hotel. We need to meet up at the one overlooking the river,' Zadie explains carefully. 'I've got the letter inviting you to the audition. All you have to do is hop on a number 15 bus and get yourself into Leeds city centre.'

I nod. I can hear Rochelle in the background. 'I need a lift!' she yells at Sharon, who's still covered in Flo's breakfast. The baby is squawking. 'It's pouring! How am I supposed to get into school in this weather?'

'OK?' Zadie asks.

Another nod from me. I haven't dared to

look in a mirror since Zadie plucked my eyebrows. All I'm likely to see is a seagull, a big mouth and two scared-rabbit brown eyes. Zadie made me get up early and wash my hair to make sure I was presentable.

'Zadie, take my keys and give Rochelle a lift into school!' Sharon yells, while Roche storms past and deliberately bangs me with her bag.

'Want to come?' Zadie asks.

I shake my head. 'I'll walk.'

'Right. See you at the hotel.' She's about to leave, but she hovers on the doorstep. 'This is your big chance, Marsha, you know that?'

Don't. I'm gonna seriously throw up if you say that!

'All you have to do is keep your nerve and follow orders. You don't have to say anything, OK?'

Lucky, that, considering the way I mangle stuff when I speak.

'You don't even have to smile. In fact, to be a model you can be medically brain dead,' Zadie assures me.

Thanks.

'Just walk up to the judges, twirl and walk away again. Let the camera do the rest.'

'I'm getting drenched!' Rochelle wails.

Inside the house, Flo squawks some more. Sharon chucks dishes in the dishwasher.

OK, so it's dead exciting and glamorous, and a secret part of me is buzzing over being invited to the fashion shoot at a posh hotel, but I'd still give a squillion quid not to go through with today. Believe me.

Three

By the time I get to school, the whole place knows.

'Good luck at the contest!' Kids I've hardly ever spoken to, like Laura White and Jade Usborne, come up to me as if we're best mates.

I go into permanent mega-blush.

'Yeah, good luck, Marsh,' Stef mutters.

Wow! My mouth falls open.

Stef's cornered me during morning break, when Laura and Jade have just started stuffing cheese and onion Kettle Chips into their mouths and I'm busy wondering how many calories there are in your average crisp, knowing that top models can't afford to pile on the pounds.

'And sorry, I've been – well, y'know,' Stef goes on.

sheepish *adjective*
embarrassed or timid
Word family: **sheepishly** *adverb*,
sheepishness *noun*

This is Stef we're talking about.

'That's OK,' I tell her. We're mates again. Relief! 'It wasn't me who entered this stupid competition in the first place,' I point out. 'This is all down to Zadie.'

Stef nods. 'How's Rochelle taking it?'

'Not good,' I murmur. 'Zadie made her lend me her jeans.'

'Ouch!' Stef winces. 'I bet she thinks it should be her up there, strutting her stuff.' She talks like one who knows.

The end-of-break bell is about to go, so I find Lisa and haul her to the staffroom with me to hand my note to Mr Adams.

'Face of the Year?' he asks, looking like

it's all a big mistake. 'Is it a beauty contest, or what?'

'Yeah, Miss World!' Lisa giggles.

'It's a competition in a magazine,' I explain in a croaky voice.

'Marsha's gonna be the next Kate Moss!' This comes from Lisa.

Thanks, pal! I wonder if blushing like a tomato is in your genes? Like sweating too much, or having a big mouth. If it is, my gene pool is totally naff.

'And your father is asking for time off school?' Mr A demands. He's about eighty years old, with a face like a walnut.

I mumble something about Zadie entering me for the contest.

'Face of the Year!' he mutters, staring right at me. 'It goes against the grain to be allowing time off for something like this. What kind of superficial standards are we fostering? What message does it send to the rest of the class?' Blah-blah. He goes off on one.

'Get real!' Lisa giggles behind his back.

Luckily other teachers are pushing past to

go to lessons, so my wizened group tutor doesn't hear.

wizened (say *wizzund*) *adjective*
withered or dried up

It comes after **wizard** and before **woad**. Words look weird after you've stared at them two or three times.

'Can I go?' I ask. I'll be crushed if he says no, which makes me realize something. Like, I can be dreading an event and making myself nearly puke with worry, but deep down, I still want to do it. Who wouldn't?

My teacher waves Dad's note in my face. 'I can hardly stop you, can I?'

When I'm rich and famous and a journalist asks me that question about which teacher had the most influence over me when I was young, it definitely won't be Mr Prune-Face Adams.

'Thanks,' I gabble, then leg it.

At the end of morning lessons I changed into jeans etcetera in the girls' loos, then made my exit when everyone was eating their sarnies. The only person I saw while I waited for the bus was boy-band gorgeous Enrique from Scott's year, who had a dentist's appointment.

He stared at my (Roche's) Diesel jeans like he knew why I had the afternoon off. He did. 'Hope you get through to the next round,' he said with a grin when I hopped on to the number 15.

'Thanks,' I said, red as a traffic light. *I won't. No way.*

Leeds city centre is scary. Everyone except me knows what they're doing and where they're going. There's a man in a top hat outside Harvey Nicks.

I skulk past and head downhill, past the Corn Exchange to the Riverside.

'You're late,' Zadie says when I find the side entrance.

There's a swish restaurant on the ground floor overlooking the river, a bit different to the school canteen.

'You're early,' I snap back. Not so much

butterflies in my stomach as dirty great jumbo jets.

'C'mon,' she says, hurrying inside.

We follow signs saying 'Face of the Year', down corridors, up in a glass lift, along more miles of carpet, until we reach the Wharfedale Suite.

'Hi!' A woman standing at a table greets us and asks for my name.

'Marsha Martinez,' Zadie tells her.

The woman hands me a badge. 'You're the last of the ten contestants to arrive. Stacey is about to start. You'll find a seat near the far end.'

I take in the room. It's huge, with big windows overlooking the city. There are rows of seats on either side of a long, low platform, nine other kids of my age, plus mums and a few dads. There's music in the background, and a loud buzz of voices.

And we have to make our way to the only empty seats, pushing past people and stumbling over bags on the floor. Not a great start, but we make it.

Then Stacey Nicholls appears on the catwalk. Stacey who writes the Ed's letter in *Dreamtime*. *'Hi girls! Welcome to the mag with the lowdown on the celebs. Find out how Gavin from Fantastix learned to live with the stresses of stardom. And don't miss our Face of the Year contest on page 32.'*

'Hi girls,' she says now – live, in the flesh. 'And welcome to the northern regional heat of *Dreamtime* magazine's Face of the Year competition!'

The buzz in the room cuts out like someone flicked a switch. We all stare at Stacey and give her ten out of ten for fashion, which makes sense when you think she's the editor on a national teen mag.

I like her make-up, which isn't over the top, and her tippety-tappety, strappy designer shoes, which are.

She smiles, and it's like she's beaming in on me and no one else. 'We've seen your pics and chosen you from the thousands who entered our competition. So congrats to you all. You're brill to have made it this far!'

Zadie digs me in the ribs and grins. She's settling in and having a cool time.

I'm not. The jumbos are still roaring around my stomach – *neeyah*!

'At *Dreamtime* we're always on the lookout for new models,' Stacey tells us. 'We have scouts in shopping centres, schools and pop concerts to find us the face that will look fab on our covers. The fashion industry is always changing, and we aim to be there, leading the way with the new look before it hits the high streets.' Pause to study our star-struck mugs. 'And that's where you come in.'

Wow. I'm beginning to believe her, I'm *wanting* to believe her. For the first time I can actually see my face on the front of the mag. I allow myself to feel a tiny flicker of hope.

'Today we want you to strut your stuff in front of top model agents and photographers, who will pick out a winner and send her on her star-studded way to the grand final.'

Zadie quickly loses interest in Stacey and

begins to scan the room for guys with cameras, trying to pick out her hero, Domenico Lane.

'But before you go off to your sessions with our *Dreamtime* hair stylists and make-up artists, here are a few dos and don'ts,' Stacey tells us. She's like a glitzy big sister, smiling down on us. '*Do* look confident up here on the catwalk, even if you don't feel it. Try to be natural. Be patient when you're waiting for your turn. *Don't* get put off by the cameras flashing. *Don't* put on a fake smile to impress us, but let your inner self come through. Most of all, *don't* be too upset if you don't win.'

I take in every word. Stacey's voice is smooth and sweet as honey.

'Not everyone is cut out to be a model,' she confides.

I glance around at the other girls. I can tell they think they are total model material, no question. They're here in their bronzing powder and curly lashes, their punk eyeliner and glossy lips.

'Hey!' Stacey brings her speech to a

close. 'This is a fun day. We're chuffed you're here, and whatever you do – win or lose – enjoy!'

'She's cool,' I said to Zadie.

'Yeah.' Zadie's eyes were out on stalks looking for Dom. We were in a queue for me to have my hair done.

The kid in front whispered to her mum that she needed the loo. The kid behind said she felt sick. That's nerves for you.

Ahead of us were two stylists armed with sprays, gels, scrunchies and scissors. Every time a girl got restyled, the queue inched forward. I was last but one.

'How shall I have my hair done?' I muttered.

'Loose,' Zadie decided, before she finally spotted Mr Big-in-Fashion-Photography and zoomed off.

'Loose?' the stylist echoed in a disappointed voice when I got to sit in the hot seat. My hair's long and dark, almost black, like I said. There's lots of it.

They sat me down and mussed me up,

gave me raspberry-red streaks on the strands that hung forward over my cheeks.

'Very cool,' the stylist said with a flourish of his comb.

I tried not to look in the mirror.

'Wow,' the woman in the clothes section said when she saw me. 'You certainly stand out.'

She said the Diesel jeans and trainers were OK, but the leather jacket had to go. Flicking through the clothes rack, she picked out a short black T-shirt with a single crimson rose printed on the chest and back.

Then I was out the other end and standing to one side as the photographers and agents lined up along the catwalk. I could see that in the distance Zadie was getting on fine with Domenico.

'I need the loo again!' the girl next to me whispered.

'No time!' The woman who'd handed me my badge when we came in was dashing around with a clipboard, checking that we were ready to strut. Someone turned up the music and shone bright lights on the narrow platform.

'Ready!' Clipboard Woman hissed.

Girl number one wobbled forward. Act natural, Stacey had said. The poor kid wore a smile straight out of the fridge freezer. As the camera lights popped she blinked and forgot to twirl. Clipboard Woman yelled at her to turn. I saw the agents scribble things in notepads and whisper.

Number two and then three went down that catwalk like they were made of wood. Stiff smiles, stiff arms and legs. No way were they having fun.

Zadie said something witty to Domenico, who laughed, then aimed and clicked.

We were up to girl number six. I was number nine. In a weird way it was starting to feel OK.

Number seven strutted and twirled. Her head floated, her hips swayed. Wow, was she confident! The judges sat up and took notice.

'She's gonna win!' the kid with the weak bladder groaned.

And d'you know, I didn't care! Suddenly my nerves vanished and I was a different person. Ahead of me were bright lights and twenty metres of catwalk. In two minutes it would all be over.

I was calm. *Calm*. All I had to do was walk down there, pose for the cameras, turn and walk back. OK, so my mouth was too big, and I had red streaks in my hair. Fifty people were staring at me. So what?

I walked out there with my head up, minus the cheesy grin.

And I just flowed, floated like I was on air, showed them the rose on my back, let the rings on my fingers flash in the blaze of light. Twenty steps and I was back to base.

Number ten followed straight on. Were they clapping me or her? Don't be such a dweeb – it was her they liked.

vain *adjective*
1. too proud of one's looks, abilities etc.
2. futile or useless
[Latin *vanus* empty]

The show was over and the rellies came

running. *You were great. You were fab. You looked really cool.*

'Wow!' Zadie said to me. 'I don't know what got into you out there, but if we could bottle it we'd make a fortune!'

Four

'Look at these,' Domenico said, while we hung around waiting for the judges to make up their minds.

Zadie had dragged Mr Big across and introduced me as her kid sister. He offered to show me the pics he'd taken of me on the catwalk.

I grimaced, but steeled myself to take a look at the little screen, at a figure in a black T-shirt with red streaks in her hair.

'Cool!' Zadie gushed.

'You stand out from the crowd, that's for sure,' Dom said.

'Is that a good or a bad thing?' I asked.

He shrugged.

'Good. You're being yourself, not a clone of someone you saw in a magazine,' Zadie insisted.

Call me suspicious, but I reckon her ucky big-sister act was put on partly for Domenico's benefit. Anyway, he seemed well impressed.

'So, Zadie, when are you gonna show me some of your work?' Domenico asked. 'I liked the one you sent in to the competition – it was well moody.'

'Is that a good or a . . . ?' I chipped in, but they weren't listening.

'When d'you reckon?' Zadie schmoozed. They drifted off in the direction of the judges' table.

'How about tonight? I have to go back to London tomorrow.'

'Where?'

'Here at the hotel. Eight o'clock.'

'Cool.'

I left them to it and looked at the table where the judging was going on. Stacey sat there with four agents, talking, looking up, nodding or shaking their heads and then talking some more.

This seemed to go on for what felt like hours, but was probably fifteen minutes, at the end of which Domenico and Zadie were practically engaged and the contents of my stomach felt like well-churned concrete.

Then I saw Stacey get Clipboard Woman to dash around asking everyone to be quiet.

'Ssh-sshhh!' she warned. 'The judges are ready to announce the result.'

Nine kids and their mums and me all held their breaths. Stacey stood up and poured her honey-sweet voice over us.

'Well,' she announced, 'there's no doubt about it, you girls from up north sure have star quality, and it's given us a hard time trying to decide which one to send forward to the national final.'

I was at the back of the room, a bit apart from Zadie and Dom, looking at the silvery, sparkly, mostly blonde opposition. I could feel the drum section from a boy band thumping away inside my chest.

'In the end we came up with two names,' Stacey confessed.

'Hu-uhh!' Ten kids let out their breaths in a synchronized groan.

suspense *noun*
a state of anxious uncertainty: 'the film kept us in *suspense* about the murderer's identity'
Word family: **suspenseful** *adjective*
[Latin *suspensus* hung up]

'I'm gonna give you the name of the runner-up first, and then the name of the winner. OK, the judges liked this contestant because of her fun quality and her confidence. And her name is . . .'

Cue extra-fast drum roll and a big blast of keyboard, all inside my ribcage.

'. . . Caiti Nelson!'

Number seven with the swishing hips yelped and covered her mouth with both hands. Then she blubbed. (Because she was happy, or because she only came second? Who knows?) Her mum hugged her.

I felt numb.

Stacey waited until Caiti had calmed down. 'But today we chose a winner with a totally original look which we reckon will take her a long way in the world of modelling. And her name is . . .'

I closed my eyes. The guitars wailed and the lead singer sang.

'. . . Marsha Martinez!'

I didn't yelp, I didn't cry. I just stood there with my mouth wide open.

Clipboard Woman grabbed me and shoved me down to the front. Domenico took my pic with Stacey and the other judges. *Pop-pop-pop*, the bulbs flashed. Everyone clapped.

Rochelle will never forgive me. I'm serious.

We came home and told everyone that I'd won. I'd already texted Lisa and Stef with the good news. **Ur not gonna believe it – i'm in the final!!!**

Sharon had to sit down to get over the shock. 'What do you mean, won?'

'Y'know, came first, beat the others, got chosen to go to London!' Sassy Zadie spelt it out.

I was still in shock.

'How much d'you win?' Scott wanted to know.

'When does she go to London?' Sharon asked, as if I wasn't there.

'This Saturday. The finals take place over the whole weekend. Don't worry, I'll go with her.' Zadie had worked it all out.

'Who pays for the hotel and the train fare?' was my stepmum's next question.

'They do. *Dreamtime* foots the bill. Stop moaning, Mum. Everything's cool.'

incredulous (say *in-kred-yoolus*) *adjective* disbelieving

I'd won. I'd actually got through!

'I thought you were going to a party in Manchester with Jude this weekend,' Sharon reminded Zadie, whose face fell for a split second.

'Yeah well, he can go by himself,' she decided, then dashed upstairs to have a shower and get ready for her date with Domenico.

'Don't think you're borrowing my jeans and trainers again,' Rochelle muttered.

There was poison in her voice, her eyes, her whole body.

spite *noun*
a malicious urge to hurt, humiliate, or annoy

'Rochelle, go to the shop for some Pampers,' Sharon ordered.

Then the kitchen was empty except for me, her and little Flo. The baby squawked, so I picked her up and walked around the room.

I was hoping that Sharon would get over the shock and say something nice, but fat chance.

'Have you told your dad yet?' she asked me in a flat voice.

I shook my head. 'I want to surprise him when he gets in,' I said a touch smugly.

So what did she do? She only went and texted him with the news before he got back.

* * *

45

'You won!' he said with a big grin that didn't hide the fact that he'd had another hard day. 'How great is that!'

My dad came up to me and gave me a big hug. 'How did it feel? Were you a bag of nerves?'

'Just a bit,' I laughed. Remember the cement mixer in my stomach. 'But Zadie was right there with me. And in the end it was pretty cool.' I wanted him to feel pleased for me, to cheer him up after work.

'Just as long as she doesn't expect us to fork out for an agent and a posh portfolio full of professional photos,' Sharon cut in. 'We can't afford that, Tony.'

'She realizes that, don't you, Marsh?'

I didn't say anything – I let it all kick off around me. I saw Dad frown and flick the switch on the kettle. Sharon was too busy changing nappies and spooning food down Flo's throat to make him a cuppa.

'Tell me more about it, Marsh,' he invited.

'Like I said, I was having kittens. Then at the last second I wasn't. I just thought, what the heck, I couldn't give a . . .'

'Marsha!' Sharon jumped in, looking daggers at me.

That was the start of it – Sharon saying she was sick of the way I talked, and Dad saying that she was always picking on me, and why couldn't she cut me a bit of slack, especially on a day like today, when I'd done something they could really be proud of.

'You call prancing down a catwalk something to be proud of?' Sharon snorted.

Flo started to snivel and then Dad gave Sharon a dirty look and she came back at him with loads of stuff about how he'd better not criticize her, and how would he like to stay in and look after the baby, day in, day out?

'Go back to work, then,' Dad said. 'Go and work in the florist's with Rochelle. We could do with the extra money.'

And then she really did kick off big-time – there was no stopping her.

I can still hear it now, sitting up in my room looking into the mirror, wondering what it's all about.

The thing is, I've heard it all before.

'You spoil Marsha rotten!' Sharon yells at the top of her voice. 'My kids don't get a look in. You never say anything nice about Rochelle. And what about Scott? When was the last time you took him to a football match?'

'Scott wouldn't be seen dead with me at a match,' is Dad's answer, and I know this is true.

'What about Rochelle, then? You're always picking on her instead of encouraging her, nagging her about schoolwork, and you never do that with precious little Ms Supermodel up there!'

Which I know is *not* true. He makes me do my homework before I watch telly.

Anyway, Dad's had enough.

I hear the door slam and his car start up in the street.

Mirror, mirror, on the wall . . .

I turn it blank side out.

It's eight o'clock and I wish I'd never entered Face of the Year.

If I hadn't won the northern heat, Sharon

wouldn't have found a reason to have a go at Dad tonight.

I wouldn't be sitting here now, feeling that my family is falling apart – *again*!

Five

'The thing is, I have to baby-mind Marsha,' Zadie explained to Jude on the phone.

She'd dragged me off to the charity shops after school on Tuesday to look for something wacky to wear. I frowned when I heard her using me to fob her boyfriend off.

'Yeah, she won her heat yesterday. I have to take her to London, so I can't make Manchester this weekend.'

Last night she'd been out with Domenico. She hadn't got home until one in the morning. I noticed she didn't tell Jude that.

Jude's a psychology student in Newcastle. He used to live down Forest Lane and went to Granby High like the rest of us. That's where Zadie first met him. They went travelling together in their gap year.

'Listen, that's the way it is. I can't do anything about it, OK?' Zadie cut the call short and came to help me flick through rails of seventies flares and eighties new-romantic tops. 'Jude's paranoid,' she muttered.

paranoia (say *parra-noya*) *noun*
a mental disorder marked by the unjustified belief that one is being persecuted, usually accompanied by megalomania and insane distrust
[Greek *paranoos* distraught]

The dictionary doesn't always help.

'He's accusing me of cheating,' Zadie huffed.

Like, yeah! I kept my mouth shut though.

'Try this on,' she suggested, holding up a leopardskin-print miniskirt. 'And this, and this.'

I ended up with a heap of trashy outfits with cutaway bits and platform heels.

51

'You wanna be different, remember.' Zadie texted her mates non-stop while I tried the clothes on. 'That's what helped you get through the heat.'

'But different in a good way,' I muttered. 'D'you want me to win this competition, or not?'

'You're twelve,' she reminded me. 'What d'you know?'

I acted stubborn and ended up with nothing from Oxfam, and just a cool chunky belt from Cancer Research.

Think we shd take a break, Jude texted.

Let's talk about it nxt wk, Zadie texted back, and shut him out of her head.

She can be hard as nails sometimes, like I said.

'Marsha, take the ironing upstairs. Marsha, make the beds. Who's been smearing chocolate over the sofa cushions. Marsha, I bet it was you!'

After I won the northern section of Face of the Year, I got it in the neck from the moment I got up to the time I went to bed.

And this wasn't just Sharon's normal Moaning Minnie routine.

For a start, she turned up the heat whenever Dad was around.

'Shall I tell you the latest?' she kicked off on the Thursday evening while we were all sitting round the table eating pasta. 'I overheard your darling Marsha telling her friend Stef on the phone that I looked old enough to be Flo's grandmother!'

I stopped sucking spaghetti into my mouth mid-slurp.

If you're wondering, did I actually say that – yeah, I did. I was well fed up with Sharon at the time.

Dad let his fork drop on to his plate and gave a sigh.

'Aren't you going to do anything about it?' Sharon challenged.

Scott and Rochelle sat back to enjoy the show.

'What?' Dad said. He's like me – not one for a lot of talking.

'Well, you could tell her it's a horrid thing to say for a start. Old enough to be Flo's grandmother!' she repeated, her voice rising and quivering.

We all stared at her. Here was a woman with dyed blonde hair that was showing grey at the roots. Her eyes were puffy from not getting enough sleep, her skin was blotchy.

So was it true, what I'd said, or not? OK, so it's not very nice, though you can tell I had my reasons. But anyway, I was still feeling guilty.

guilty (say *gil-tee*) *adjective*
1. having done wrong: 'we all knew he was *guilty*, despite his objections'
2. feeling or showing guilt: 'she had a *guilty* conscience after she lied to her mother'

Wow, does that look weird now? Sometimes I think I obsess over words because it keeps me separate from the nasty stuff going on around me.

'Just take no notice,' Dad told Sharon wearily, with a sideways glance at me.

Wrong! Sharon went off on one.

'You always take her side!' she screeched.

You heard him. He didn't, did he?

'No, I don't.'

'You do. Rochelle, Scott – you heard what he said. I asked him for some back-up, and what do I get? Nothing. Not a scrap of support. And meanwhile, Marsha sits there all smug, smiling and enjoying every second!'

I don't know if I looked smug. I don't think I was smiling.

'It's since she got through to that final,' Rochelle said. She knows how to stir bigtime. 'She really thinks she's it!'

'Huh, and you don't!' I said with a massive dollop of irony.

irony (say *eye-ra-nee*) *noun*
1. a mockingly humorous use of words in which the intended meaning is the opposite of what is actually said
2. a situation which seems to mock reasonable hopes: 'by an *irony* of fate he died just before he was going to alter his will in my favour'
[Greek *eironeia* understatement or pretended ignorance]

* * *

Sharon agreed with Rochelle and ran with it. 'Yes, Tony, that contest is the worst thing you ever let her do. From now on, she'll be even more out of control than before. In fact, I think you should make her pull out. Tony, are you listening? Make Marsha withdraw from that stupid competition, or . . .'

He sat staring at her like she was an alien from outer space – like he'd just realized what kind of monster he'd married. It had taken ages for the light to flick on inside his head, but it looked like right now, at that moment, he saw everything in a new, crystal-clear way. '. . . Or what?' he said, deathly quiet.

Sharon realized she'd boxed herself into a corner and wimpily sidestepped. 'Don't you think you should at least punish her for the way she speaks to me?'

'I don't know. I wasn't there,' Dad said.

'I was,' Roche chipped in.

Liar! She'd been nowhere near.

'Marsha had it in for Mum. She knew what she said was well out of order.'

That's when the tears started, and Sharon jumped up from the table. She dashed out.

Crying's like a skin rash – it spreads. First Sharon, then Flo, then me. Yeah, call me sad, but I blubbed big-time. I couldn't think of enough hard words to keep me busy.

Rochelle stayed dry-eyed though. She leaned over to mutter something to Scott and they both laughed.

But they weren't laughing half an hour later, when Sharon came and hoiked Flo out of her highchair and said she was off to her sister Helen's house.

Dad was doing the washing-up. From the back he looked a bit slumped and hunched, like the whole thing had got to be too much.

My heart did a flip and missed a beat when I saw it.

'Did you hear me?' Sharon screeched. 'I said, I've packed a bag and I'm taking Flo to Helen's.'

He still didn't react.

'Don't try to contact me,' she said, with Flo squatting on one hip as she ripped drawers open to collect bibs and other baby stuff.

Roche had drifted in from the telly room. She took in what was happening and backed out without saying a word.

It wasn't the first time this going-to-Helen's thing had happened.

'I mean it,' Sharon said, heading for the door. 'I can't take any more. I'm going to Helen's and she'll help me decide what to do.'

The fact that Dad still had his back to her must have been the final straw.

'I'm not coming back, Tony,' she said, suddenly calm and much quieter. 'I don't care what you say or what you do, this is it – I'm leaving you.'

And me. And Roche, Scott and Zadie, as it happens.

Bang – she was out of that door.

We were left standing there, totally gobsmacked.

'Dad?' I said after about five minutes of silence, going on for eternity.

* * *

Well, he played it down like he always does.

We watched telly and when Zadie came in we told her what had happened. Then we went to bed. We got up next morning. Dad came up to my room before he left for work, which was unusual for him these days.

'How much do you want for your train fare to London?' he asked.

'Nothing. It's paid for.' I hadn't slept much, I have to admit. I'd spent the whole night wondering if Dad was OK and making promises to myself that I'd stop being nasty to my stepmum. When she came back. *If* she came back. 'Shall I still go?' I asked.

'Sure,' he nodded. 'You know what Sharon's like. She goes over the top at times.'

'Don't we all?' I tried to joke. 'It's a girl thing.'

'Must be,' he mumbled, making the effort to grin.

I felt like my heartstrings were stretching and snapping in two. 'Will she change her mind?' I asked.

Dad nodded. 'Happy families, eh?'

I wanted to throw my arms around him and give him a hug. I wanted to say he was a great dad and didn't deserve all this hassle. But I didn't. 'Wish me luck, then,' I said instead.

'Good luck, Marsh. Make sure to stick with Zadie all the time you're in London, and call me if there's a slip-up of any kind.'

'Yeah, yeah. There won't be. See you on Sunday night.'

He nodded. 'Gotta go,' he said.

Clickety-click, *clickety-click*, the inter-city train carried us like a bullet aimed at the London Eye.

Good luck, Marsh! Lisa texted. Her brother just got a hundred hours of community service.

See u later, Zadie texted Domenico.

Thanks! I texted Lisa back.

Clickety-click. Out in the countryside, cows ate grass.

We pulled into King's Cross at seven-thirty. *The train terminates here. Please take all your personal belongings with you.*

Everyone else on the train was treating this as no big deal, like they travelled to London every day. They got up and lifted down briefcases, zipped up jackets, stared out of the window as the train ground to a halt.

But me – I'd already got the jitters ahead of tomorrow.

OK, so I'd won the northern heat, but what if that was a fluke? What if all the judges had needed glasses and only saw me as a blur? In which case, this was all a big mistake!

Tomorrow morning I would get to the final and they'd be different judges and they would all have their lenses in. They'd take one look at me and think, *Whoa, who let this one in?*

'Are you coming, or what?' Zadie asked.

We were the last to leave Coach C. She was standing on the platform, looking up at me. A grey tide of people shuffled by.

Then, *bam!*

'Yeah, Marsha, move your fat backside!' a voice said from behind.

I swung round and smacked Rochelle in the stomach with my bag.

Yeah, *that* Rochelle.

'Watch it!' she said, then, 'What are you staring at?'

'You. What are you doing here?' I practically had to pinch myself to make sure I wasn't having a bad dream.

'I'm coming with you, what's it look like?' Rochelle flung back at me. She barged past and jumped down on to the platform.

This was when Zadie stepped in with the explanations. 'She rang Mum and asked if she could come,' she told me. 'Mum was the one who said yes. It wasn't down to me.'

'Why?' I bleated. 'I mean, why?' Spending time with me was usually the last thing my darling stepsister wanted to do.

Rochelle grinned up at me. Her reason was typical. 'Why should you have a weekend in London, and not me?'

'Yeah, but . . .' My tongue tied up in knots, my heart raced. Clumsily I climbed down from the carriage. 'You should've told me you were on the train,' I croaked.

She was all smiles, dancing along the platform ahead of us. 'And spoil a great surprise? You should see the look on your face, Marsha!'

No thanks. 'OK, you can come to the hotel and hang around. But don't think you can muscle your way into the Face of the Year!' I mumbled.

Then I took another look at her, and saw with a terrible sinking feeling in the pit of my stomach that, whatever I said, however much I wanted her to butt out, muscling her way into Face of the Year was exactly, precisely, one hundred per cent what Rochelle planned to do.

Six

'Which of the following phrases means "affectionate"? Is it a) huffy-puffy, b) soupy-doopy, c) lovey-dovey, or d) hurly-burly?' the quiz show host asked.

Some woman on telly won a hundred quid.

'Boring!' Rochelle decided. With a flick of the remote we were bang in the middle of open-heart surgery.

'Ergh!' I couldn't look at the slimy, blubbery, bloody stuff. 'Flick back!' I pleaded.

'Wimp.' Ignoring me as usual, she used the zoom button and settled in to enjoy the gore fest.

I got up from my bed and wandered into the bathroom. This hotel was cool. It had mini-bottles of shampoo and shower gel, stacks of clean white towels. Oh, and a big mirror over the basin.

Mirror, mirror, on the wall.

'Staring at yourself won't make any difference!' Roche sniggered from the bedroom. She has this knack of tuning into the way I'm thinking. 'You're stuck with what you were born with, poor you!'

This was her tactic for boosting my confidence ahead of the final of Face of the Year.

But before that we'd had the party with the other finalists.

We'd made it out of King's Cross and hired a taxi to take us to the hotel. This was my first time in London, except for once when we'd flown to America from Heathrow when Mum was still with us, and then all I'd seen was the train station, the tube and the airport.

It felt like Leeds, only bigger, busier,

dirtier. We sat in a traffic jam for half an hour, then hopped out of the taxi into a massive marble hotel reception hall.

'What's this?' I'd asked Zadie after we'd fiddled around at the desk and signed in. I held up a plastic card inside a cardboard envelope.

'It's the key, stupid,' Rochelle had said.

I mean, how was I to know that it had a magnetic code and you slid it into the slot above the door handle?

Rochelle had chosen the best bed in a room that was crammed with a wardrobe, a desk, a table, two armchairs, a telly and twin beds plus a kid's fold-up one. Guess which one I got stuck with.

I'd unpacked when the phone went. Zadie answered it and told me we had to go back down to have dinner with the other finalists. 'The only problem is, I've just arranged to meet Dom,' she'd frowned.

'Dom'! How friendly was that all of a sudden!

'I thought you were supposed to be my minder,' I'd pointed out. No way was I going down to dinner by myself.

That was when Rochelle had jumped in, quick as a rat down a drainpipe. 'No problem, I'll look after you!'

I'd stared from her to Zadie and back. Like, throw a sardine to a piranha fish, why don't you?

'It's OK, I'll lie about my age. I'll say I'm seventeen. No one will know.' Roche has iron willpower and never takes no for an answer. Think bulldozer.

Zadie had taken about 0.2 seconds to agree. Then she'd put on her slinkiest, strappiest silver top and sailed off on her date.

Which had left me and Roche to bicker our way down to the dining room, and that was when I got really scared.

Picture a room full of mini Mary-Kate-and-Ashleys – wispy, long, streaky, breeze-ruffled hair; huge blue eyes that look like deep, dark pools; wafer-thin arms and legs. They're all sitting round the table with glamorous mums who look about twenty-five years old. They stare at me and Rochelle for a split second then decide there's no contest. They switch their perma-smiles back to each other.

'Sit!' Roche commands.

I'm weak at the knees, so I obey.

I'm next to a pushy-mum type.

Mum: So, which heat did you win through in?

Me: The north.

Mum: (smiles pityingly) Melody won the heat for London and the south east.

Melody: What's it like in the north? Is it really freezing?

You get the picture. My voice sounds flat – I'm definitely a poor little sardine out of water.

It gets worse. The mums talk about signing their kids up with agents, and how many shoots Melody/Liberty/Janine/Kelly have already done. They look ahead dreamily to deals with New Look, when Melody/Liberty/Janine ... will have their faces smiling out of every High Street window in the universe.

I play with the food on my plate. What *is* gnocchi? Whatever it is, I wish I hadn't ordered it.

Roche doesn't help. She tells Melody's
mum that Zadie only sent in my photo for
a laugh, and no one can believe I got this
far.

Then the woman I recognize as Ms
Clipboard from the Riverside stands up at
the far end of the table and announces the
schedule for the weekend.

'Remember me? I'm Verity. Tomorrow is
gonna be fun!' she tells us – like, *tells* us –
fun, or else! 'We'll be shooting at one of the
city's most famous landmarks, taking you
up in the London Eye and getting you to
pose for our photographers in one of those
wonderful glass pods. The whole of London
will be spread out beneath your feet!'

Melody and the glam gang ooh and aah.

'I can't stand heights!' I whisper to myself.
My stomach flips and churns the gnocchi
into a pulp.

Ms Clipboard lets the noise die down then
tells us about Sunday.

'Madame Tussauds!' she announces.
'Another cool location, where you can rub
shoulders with the world's most famous

celebs. Hook up with Brad Pitt, schmooze with JLo, meet Madonna!'

Wow! Even I'm impressed. I'm gonna meet the stars!

Until Rochelle reminds me that Madame Tussauds is full of waxwork dummies and the celebs aren't real.

'Yeah, I know!' I mutter back.

'We'll hand out printed sheets with exact times and venues,' Verity tells us. 'Make sure that you arrive at the location two hours before the shooting and judging begins. That gives time for the stylists to work their usual magic.'

Mums take note and scribble things in their organizers. Rochelle flirts with a waiter.

Melody leans over to Janine, whispers something and smirks. Liberty talks to Kelly. I'm out in the cold with my butterfly stomach and too-big mouth.

'Crème brûlée?' the waiter asks me.

And I haven't a clue what he means.

Which brings me up to date with the heart

surgery and Rochelle scoffing the Kettle Chips and me throwing a wobbler in front of the bathroom mirror.

Roche must have got bored with bypasses, because I heard the telly volume go lower, and then she wandered in to join me.

'Hey!' I objected, trying to shove her out and bolt the door.

Bulldozer girl slammed the lid down and sat on the loo. 'This is a right mess,' she began in a wavery voice, looking like she wanted to fess up.

'What is?' This was my big mistake – to treat her like a normal person and invite her to carry on talking.

'Mum and Tony, the whole marriage thing.'

Thud. My heart hit my boots. This was one thing I did not want to talk to Rochelle about. 'Oh, it'll be cool,' I bleated, Dad-like. Who was I trying to kid?

'No, it won't.' Rochelle grabbed a strip of loo paper and blew her nose. 'I was talking to Mum earlier.'

'When?'

incredulous (say *in-kred-yoolus*)

No, I've already done that one. Anyway, look it up and don't expect so much help from me.

'Earlier!' Roche snapped. 'She was having a real go about Tony, how he never helped with the baby, and all that stuff.'

'I know,' I muttered, then I took a deep breath. Why was Roche talking like this now, like she really cared? What did she expect me to do about it?

I should've said, 'Don't tell me. I don't want to know what your mum said about my dad.'

'Well, it's true,' she went on. 'He's always away in Spain, buying tiles – ha ha!'

The *ha ha* annoyed me. I fiddled with the mini-bottles of shower gel, keeping my back to her.

She ignored my huffy silence. 'Mum says she doesn't trust him. He *says* he's buying tiles, but he's probably got a girlfriend over in Bilbao. That's why he spends so much time there.'

I shot out of the bathroom and turned the telly back on. *La-la-la, I'm not listening!*

Bump-bump-bump – the red heart throbbed under the surgeon's white rubber gloves. Gore fest, like I said.

'Listen!' Rochelle had followed me. She stood in front of the screen. 'Your dad's cheating on Mum. She found out.'

'No way!' I turned on her, practically spitting out the words.

'He is. She did.'

Don't expect great dialogue from either of us at this point. We were both so mad we could hardly speak.

'Prove it!' I yelled.

'Oh, grow up!' Rochelle was laughing, actually laughing! 'That's what happens in real life – couples cheat on each other! Anyway, like it or not, Mum's gonna ditch Tony for good this time.'

'Good!' *Definitely, definitely Good!*

'You won't say that when she's taken Flo away and never lets him see her again!'

Bump-bump-bu-bump! The heart in the background missed a beat. Or was it mine?

'She can't do that!' I cried.

'Listen,' she said again, talking slowly now. 'I'll only say this once – I spoke to Mum, she's had enough. On Sunday morning, when Tony's out playing golf, she's gonna sneak back to the house, get the locks changed and refuse to let him back in!'

'She can't *do* that!'

Rochelle smirked. 'You don't believe me, do you?'

'No way! You're just saying it to make me feel bad because you want me to look a wreck and lose the contest. You never even talked to your mum about it!'

'Did.'

'Didn't! When? I never heard you. You're making it up!'

Rochelle shrugged and plonked herself down on her bed, opened a mag and started to flick through. 'Please yourself.'

It was like a bomb had dropped and demolished my life. There was rubble and dust everywhere. I didn't know which way to run.

'You're just jealous!' I yelled.

'Yeah, yeah.'

'You wish it was you who was in the final! You think you're it, and you're not, with your blonde streaks and stupid Diesel jeans!'

Rochelle laughed again.

We were in a hotel room in the middle of London. There was nowhere for me to go. I ran into the bathroom and this time I bolted the door.

Turn on the shower, step under it, feel the hot water prickle my skin.

Forget Rochelle. Blank out what she'd said. She was a liar, a mean, stupid liar!

I never gave her the satisfaction of seeing me cry.

That night I lay on my kid's camp-bed staring up at the ceiling. Still no sign of Zadie at two in the morning. I planned getting up as soon as it was light, taking my train ticket and shooting back up to Leeds, to tell Dad every word Rochelle had said.

OK, so I would miss Face of the Year and the London Eye, but I would be saving Dad's marriage, wouldn't I?

He would phone Sharon at her sister's place, explain that it was getting out of hand and that he needed to talk to her. They would be able to patch things up.

You'll miss the contest! I reminded myself. *And that's exactly what Rochelle wants!*

It hit me so hard that I sat up on my rickety bed. This was her way, not only of making me lose, but of getting me out of the contest, the poisonous toad!

To upset me so much over Sharon and Dad that I couldn't face the Eye and Madame Tussauds.

To get to me and make me feel like my world had fallen apart. And all the time she was making it up and laughing behind my back.

Can people be that mean?

They can if they're three years older than you and they hate your guts. They think they're prettier, cleverer, more trendy, more everything than you, and then they see you getting a chance to die for.

Face of the Year, mega fashion deals, international jet-setting, fame!

So I decided to blank out what Rochelle had told me and not even give her the satisfaction of phoning Dad to warn him. Instead, I would concentrate on the contest. *I'll wear my hair up this time*, I decided. *Not so smooth and hanging over my face, more rock chick, with lots of volume.*

Call me shallow, but that's how I got out of the hole Rochelle had dumped me in.

Zadie came creeping in at about three and got her head down for a few hours' kip.

By eight o'clock I was calm enough to get up, draw the curtains and look out over London at that big wheel by the river, the skyscrapers, and the snaking silver track of the Thames in the early morning light.

Seven

'I'm as corny as Kansas in August

  High as the flag on the Fourth of July

  Dee-dah, dee-dee-dah, dah-dum-dum, dah-dah-da

  . . . I'm in love, I'm in love, I'm in love with a wonderful guy!'

  Zadie was in the bathroom, singing along to an ancient cowboy musical on the Movie Channel. It was 9.00 am on a brilliant sunny day.

  Rochelle was still a lump under the duvet, blocking her ears.

  'I am. I'm in love!' Zadie swanned back into our bedroom wrapped in a big white towel. She'd had six hours' sleep and looked fresh as a shampoo advert.

I hadn't slept at all and felt like death. And this was my big day, remember.

'Dom's such a funny guy!' Zadie sighed, shaking out her wet hair all over me. 'He's so witty, and he knows movies I've never even heard of. You should hear him talk about the films of Jean Luc Godard.'

'No thanks,' the Lump grunted.

What happened to Jude? I wondered. *Did he suddenly vanish from the face of the earth?*

'He took me to a French restaurant – nouvelle cuisine. Then on to a club. We sat and talked for hours!'

'Are you gonna get up, or what?' I asked Rochelle. We had to be at the Eye in an hour and a half.

'If you'll excuse
The expression I use
I'm in love with a wonderful guy!'

Zadie trilled, drying her hair, stepping into her clothes and being generally mega annoying.

At last Roche crawled out from under the

bedclothes. 'How old is this Domenico?' she wanted to know.

'Thirty-two,' Zadie said.

'Ergh, that's disgusting!' Roche groaned, rolling out of bed.

'How long will it take to get to the Eye?' I asked, to change the subject. I didn't want Zadie and Rochelle having a massive row and making us late.

Zadie looked at her watch. 'Depends on the tube. C'mon, let's get a move on!'

'What about breakfast? I haven't had a shower. Give me a chance to do my hair.' Roche made a million excuses and went at a snail's pace.

'Right, I'm off!' I decided at 9.30, and I was out of the door before she could stop me, with Zadie charging after, and Rochelle still inside the room in her bra and pants.

Down in reception, Zadie and I bumped into Marie Walker, one of the other finalists I haven't mentioned yet, and her mum.

'Share a taxi?' the mum offered, and so the four of us jumped in a black cab and shunted through the traffic towards the river.

I sat wearing my stroppy look next to Marie.

'God, I feel sick!' she groaned, while cars and lorries spewed out exhaust fumes and bike riders with masks over their mouths wove through the gaps.

Weird, but that one sentence made me like Marie. 'Me too,' I sighed, glad to share.

Marie: I didn't sleep!

Me: Me neither.

Marie: I never thought it would be this bad.

Me: Me neither.

Yep, I was my usual scintillating self as far as conversation went.

'Stop moaning, you two!' Zadie said.

I think my new mate, Marie, deserves a proper description.

She's as tall as me, which is nearly five nine. She's got short brown hair which flops over her face in a feathery way, a little nose with a turned up end, quite big mouth, like me, and a really long neck. But you wouldn't look at her and straightaway think 'Model!'

'How come you're in the final?' she asked me, not in a nasty way.

We crossed a bridge and looked down at the sludgy brown river. 'Zadie entered for me,' I told her.

And it turned out that it was Marie's mum who had sent in her pic. They live in Stirling, in Scotland.

'I do a bit of modelling myself,' Mrs Walker chipped in. 'For catalogues and stuff. Not exactly Elle McPherson or anything.'

Marie raised her eyebrows. 'They don't seem to realize what this competition stuff does to us. I'm a wreck!'

'Me too.' I was grinning now, and feeling more relaxed as the taxi pulled up in the big space below the Eye, which, by the way, is ginormous and dead cool. It's bigger than anything else around, made of steel, with these oval, see-through pods hanging from the rim. Each pod fits about fifteen people, I reckon. There was a queue of at least two hundred snaking across the concourse.

We piled out of the taxi, paid the fare and headed for the *Dreamtime* caravan, parked near the ticket office, where we would find Ms Clipboard and her army of stylists.

Plus five other finalists, which with me and Marie made seven altogether. All crammed into a silver caravan like the ones film crews use on location. It was hot in there, I can tell you.

We did all the stuff we did last time in the regional heats, without the Stacey welcome. That happens tonight at dinner, after we've finished shooting at the Eye.

Another thing that was different about this final was that *all* the other girls already had experience.

'I was spotted at a school fashion show actually,' Janine says to Melody as they sit down in the make-up chairs. On goes the blusher and lippy. 'I'm on the books at the Choice agency.'

Melody closes her eyes for eyeshadow. 'I've done *Mizz* twice. It was cool.'

Marie's eyebrows shoot up under her

feathery fringe. I pull a sour-lemon face. These kids are twelve going on thirty.

Brush-flick-squeeze-squirt! The hair stylist froofs up Kelly's auburn hair. 'Who's your agent?' Kelly asks Liberty, who has little blonde knobbles sticking out in all directions – very attractive!

Liberty gives Kelly a name that I've never heard of.

'Wow,' says Kelly. 'They've got Elle McPherson on their books.'

I sigh and Marie's eyebrows work overtime. We're standing in line, waiting for our outfits. Marie gets given a bright pink top with white stripes down the side and a huge silver logo that says 'DO YOU KNOW WHO I AM?' There's a silver miniskirt to go with it.

'Do I have to?' she protests.

Me? I get a black string vest thing to wear over a red T-shirt, with baggy black trousers – quite cool, actually. Black and red again, but not so weird. They give me two black sweatbands decorated with red stars. I decide to wear them both on one arm.

'Wow!' Liberty and Melody chorus when

they see Marie and me emerge from
the changing cubicles. Not 'Wow!' as in
'Hey, that's cool!' But 'Wow!', as in 'You
poor things. Fancy them making you wear
that!'

Liberty is in a white zip-up cardigan with
a fluffy, fake-fur front. Melody looks like a
rainbow in a naff multi-coloured T-shirt.
Miaow!

When all the spraying and brushing is
finished, they say we can leave the caravan.
Together, making a grand entrance for the
benefit of people in the long queue, and so
the photographers can capture us all in a
group.

Liberty stands on my foot as she pushes
to the front. I take a deep breath, catch sight
of myself in a mirror looking moody, with
two long straggles of hair loose over my
cheeks and the rest pulled back high to one
side of my head.

'Good luck,' Marie whispers in her 'DO YOU
KNOW WHO I AM?' top.

'Yeah, good luck,' I say, and I mean it.

* * *

I'm up in a pod and remembering how scared I am of heights.

I'm by myself with Domenico and his camera lens, the fifth contestant to go up in the London Eye.

'Look natural,' he tells me.

I can't. I'm standing on a metal floor surrounded by glass. I'm hundreds of feet off the ground inside a giant transparent egg. There's the Houses of Parliament and Big Ben. There's St Paul's. *Whoa!*

The wheel turns and the pod rises even higher. The streets and river are laid out like a map, like at the start of *EastEnders*.

'Turn this way, Marsha!' Dom is standing on the bench to get an unusual angle. He's pointing his camera and waiting for me not to look terrified.

Let me out! I stare at the camera, hear a click. The pod shudders and moves on.

'Your sister Zadie's an interesting girl,' Domenico says in a casual, joking sort of way, as if to take my mind off things. *Click-click.*

'How d'you mean?'

'Dead keen on her photography, for a start.' *Click*. Dom's dressed in a battered leather jacket and black T-shirt. He's losing his hair, so he's shaved what's left and wears a stud in one ear. 'She's got a lot to learn though.'

'About photography?' I ask. I'm forgetting that I'm a mile above the city in an egg.

Dom grins. *Click-click*. 'Yeah.'

I don't think he's saying what he means. I think there's something beneath the surface. 'She thinks you're cool,' I tell him.

He grins again. 'That's better, Marsha. Now we're working well. Turn away, put your hands on your hips, head down a bit, give me one of those scowls!' *Click*.

I picture Zadie singing about Kansas while she's in the shower. 'She thinks you're *really* cool,' I insist.

'Yeah well, don't mention it to my wife,' he quips.

Wife? I look stunned.

'Stacey,' he tells me, dead matter of fact. More clicks.

'You're married!' I gasp.

'To Stacey Nicholls,' he nods. 'And listen, you can do Zadie a favour; tell her not to throw herself at guys she thinks can help her career. It'll get her a bad name.'

By this time we're over the top of the curve and heading downwards. Domenico has taken all the shots he needs.

'But she thought . . .' I begin. 'I mean, she didn't . . .'

'I know,' he grins then sighs.

We don't say any more, not even when we finally reach the platform and step out of the pod.

There's a lot I don't understand.

Like, why can't Zadie see that Dom is blanking her out this morning? She's chatting and being girly, asking him what's the best make of digital camera, and what about the ones that shoot video as well as stills? He's busy talking to Ms Clipboard and not giving Zadie much space.

Second, how come Rochelle's being nice to me? She's shown up at last and is asking me how it's going and letting everyone know that she's dead proud of her little sis for getting this far in the contest. Ms Bulldozer might con the agency scouts who are hovering outside the caravan, but she doesn't fool me. Ah yeah; the agency scouts. They're smiling at Rochelle, chatting with her. Now I get it! She's being nice to me so she gets noticed by the scouts.

Third, and this is the big one that bugs me – when something is really bad at home, and there's lots of reasons why you might want your dad to yourself and never to see your stepmum ever again, then why do you still want them to stay together and for things not to change?

Because, dummy, you'd never see your baby sister again!

Baby Flo. Yeah, there's the yucky napples and spotty bum, there's the teething and spitting out food. But Flo can crawl now, and if you let her grab hold of your fingers, she can pull herself up and stand. She's a bit wobbly, but she can do it. Also, she has thick dark hair, like me. And like Dad. She's a Martinez. She's my flesh and blood.

But remember, *Rochelle was only saying that stuff about Sharon changing the locks to scare you. It isn't true.*

'You OK?' Marie comes and asks me. She's been up in the pod, and now it's Kelly's turn. Dom pushes past Zadie to go and take more pictures.

'Yeah,' I nod. Then I frown and take my new mate to one side. 'Marie, my big sister fancies Domenico, but I just found out he's married. D'you think I should tell her?'

Marie looks up at the pod slowly rising with Kelly and Dom inside. 'Yeah,' she says, coming over all agony-aunt. 'You have to stop her from getting hurt by that love-rat, and if you don't tell her, I will!'

Eight

The pod shoot took up most of Saturday, and everyone was so busy that, despite Marie's advice, I put off talking to Zadie about Mr Zoom Lens until we were back at the hotel.

In any case, worrying about Rochelle took up a lot of my time, and meant I couldn't concentrate on the Zadie problem.

'So, Rochelle,' the scout from Choice Model Agency said, 'we could be on the lookout for seventeen-year-old girls, as well as the ones at the younger end of the age range.'

She's fifteen, not seventeen! I wanted to point out.

'Yeah well, I've done some modelling before,' Roche lied.

The woman wore a plastic badge which said Melanie Duchamp. She looked interested. 'Here's my card. Maybe you'd bring your portfolio to my office, and we could take it from there.'

'What portfolio?' I asked, once Rochelle and I had set off for the tube station. Zadie had insisted on staying behind to have coffee with Domenico, even though I'd tried to make her read my mind, silently yelling a big *N-O, don't do it!* at her. My telepathy let me down though.

telepathy (say *te-leppa-thee*)
It's where you try to transfer thoughts from your own head to someone else's

Don't do it! I was thinking when Zadie suggested the cosy coffee. But she wasn't tuned in.

'The portfolio Zadie's gonna mock up for me,' Rochelle grinned now. 'She can take the pics and I'll put fake labels in about the magazines they appeared in.'

Honest, some people stoop so low! We were halfway down the escalator and I just lost it. I gave her a look that could've killed and darted ahead, reaching the bottom before her. I hit a crowd of people surging in the opposite direction. When I came out the other side, I turned round and saw that Roche had vanished.

Later she said it was accidentally, but I didn't believe her.

Anyway, I was stranded deep under London, clutching a ticket to Pimlico, without a clue how to get there. Worse: it was my own stupid fault.

At first, I pretended I wasn't lost. I walked on until I came to a map, but the criss-crossing coloured lines didn't make sense and I couldn't find the stop I wanted.

This is when I began to panic. I turned around and went up the escalator, to start again. There must be a better map up there by the machines that let you through the barrier. But there was only the same map as the one at the bottom. I found myself taking short, shallow breaths, *Help!*

Two women pushed in front of me and talked in a foreign language, stabbing their fingers at the point on the map that was filthy and worn.

So that was where we were now. I watched the women go off to a booth and buy their tickets. After a bit I joined the queue, came up to the window and said the sentence I'd been rehearsing for the last five minutes. 'Can you tell me how to get to Pimlico, please.'

The Underground man flashed out a list of names.

I nodded and went away, keeping them in my head.

Down the escalator, then follow the signs, getting jostled, ignoring the man playing a saxophone, deciding whether to turn left or right. Short breaths, feeling a bit faint, waiting for the train. Squeezing on, studying the map above people's heads, counting the stations, then hopping off and starting over again, looking for the next line.

I did it in the end, coming up the last escalator at Pimlico, panicking again because I thought I'd lost my ticket, finding it, slotting it into the machine and coming out into the stale air of the street.

Phew! That was my first ever solo trip on the London Underground. Nightmare. And people in a million offices do this twice a day!

So now I had to find the hotel without looking like an idiot. Cross the street, then first left, second right, the woman on the newspaper stall told me.

I did what she said, sweaty now, and looking lousy, I bet. I tell you, I practically fell through the hotel doors into reception, where I found Rochelle waiting for me.

'What kept you?' were the first words she said.

So my weekend wasn't going well so far. I'd been lost on the Underground. Rochelle was getting up my nose big-time. Oh, and I was about to be made homeless.

Figure it out – if Rochelle was right and Sharon did change the locks and ditch

Dad, I went with him. Out on the streets.

She's lying! I kept on telling myself.

Rochelle would catch me glaring at her, smirk and carry on reading her mag. Or she would be texting somebody, or sounding off about being on the books of Choice. 'Melanie Duchamp signed me up the minute she saw me,' she told Mrs Walker. 'Everyone knows this Face of the Year garbage is just for little kids. It's not the kind of stuff that really matters.'

Marie's mum gave a stiff smile and walked away.

'Is that right – about Rochelle and Choice?' Marie asked me. We were hanging about in reception waiting for our evening meal.

I shook my head.

'Does she always lie?'

I nodded.

'Why?'

I'd never asked myself the question. 'Habit?' I suggested. 'Y'know, she does it so much, she doesn't even know she's doing it.'

'Yeah, but what's she trying to prove?' Maybe there's something about the water they drink in Stirling that makes Marie smarter than most kids our age.

'That she's the best,' I decided. 'She always has to have the biggest ice-cream, the best seat in the cinema, the trendiest hair style . . .'

Mirror, mirror, on the wall . . .

I don't know why, but the stupid fairytale about Snow White keeps on flitting through my head. The one where the wicked stepmother (yeah!) wants to be the most beautiful person in all the land, and the mirror keeps on telling her she isn't, that Snow White is fairest of them all, so Stepma sets out to banish the kid, then when that doesn't work, she goes off in disguise to try and poison her.

Well, in my case, there's the stepmum from hell, *plus* the stepsister. Like a double whammy. Anyway, I'm thinking red, shiny poisonous apples here.

Marie listened. 'I feel kind of sorry for Rochelle, and I definitely wouldn't want to be inside her head,' she said quietly. Then, 'Hey, did you tell Zadie about that scumbag photographer yet?'

scum *noun*
1. a layer of impure or waste matter on a liquid
2. something worthless or vile
Word family: **scum** (**scummed**, **scumming**) *verb* a) to become covered with scum b) to remove scum, **scummy** *adjective* a) covered with scum b) worthless

Scumbag isn't in the dictionary, but you get the general idea.

As it turned out, I wished I had told Zadie about Domenico, and let everyone know the score.

This bit happens fast, people jump to the wrong conclusion and it might be hard to follow.

First, Domenico Lane zooms up to the hotel entrance in his car and Zadie hops out.

Rochelle clocks the sporty number and the

fact that Zadie and Dom seem to have got very lovey-dovey. She flings down her mag on to the low table, looks at Dom's car, watches Zadie lean in through the window and say something, frowns and turns to stare at me.

I'm sitting opposite, across the table from Rochelle, still weak from my adventure on the tube. 'What?' I ask.

She refuses to answer.

Then Zadie dashes in through the automatic door and straight to the lift.

'Hmm.' Rochelle makes a noise midway between a steam engine and an angry bee.

'What!' I can see I'm not going to get an answer. Roche is thinking, and she can't talk at the same time. Multi-tasking is not her thing.

So I spring up with the feeling that a) Roche is planning a nasty surprise, and b) something bad has happened to Zadie.

I'm right both times. When I follow Zadie up in the lift and catch up with her in our room, she's flung herself face down on the bed and is crying like a baby.

'What happened?' I ask, already guessing the answer.

'Dom dumped me,' she sobs.

Honest, she goes for a drink with him twice and now acts like she's heartbroken. But don't feel too sorry for her – she's been ignoring Jude, remember. 'Forget him,' I advise.

'Easy for you to say,' she chokes. 'You're not old enough to know what it feels like.'

Thanks! 'You need someone your own age,' I point out. *Someone like Jude*.

Zadie goes on choking and snotting into the pillow. 'I'll never meet anyone like Dom again. He's so clever and cool . . .'

'. . . And married,' I drop in. Then I get to tell her what I should have told her hours earlier.

Thanks to this latest crisis, Zadie and I managed to miss our dinner.

She'd done a bit more crying and then a lot of swearing. I'd told her everything I knew about Dom and Stacey. She'd sat up on the bed, sniffed hard, chucked soggy tissues across the room, then stomped off to have a shower.

I was still getting over the whole thing when Dad rang me.

'Hey, Marshy,' he began. 'How did today go?'

'Cool,' I said. 'I'm not gonna win though.'

Dad laughed, sounding a long way off. 'Typical of you to put yourself down. But just think, my little Marshmallow all alone in London, hobnobbing with all those important people.'

'I'm not all alone. I'm with Zadie and Rochelle,' I told him.

Rochelle was news to him. 'I thought she was at Helen's with Sharon.'

I said I wished she was. No point hiding that from him, though I was biting my tongue hard about Sharon and the door locks because I didn't want to scare him without good reason. 'How you getting on?' I asked.

'The house feels pretty empty,' Dad admitted. 'Even Scott went off to his mate's. I rang Sharon, but she's not answering her phone. Give her another twenty-four hours though, and I expect she'll be ready to come home.'

'Yeah,' I said uneasily.

'You OK?'

'Yeah.'

I love Dad to bits, but he's not easy to talk to. He always wants things to be fine, even when we both know they're not. Like, he keeps a cheerful face on. To be honest, he did that when Mum left. I was seven at the time. She met Jose in a place called Santander in northern Spain, on a trip to do with business, because she and Dad had set up the tile company together. Anyway, it was ages ago and I'm totally OK with it. Dad kept me and the house and everything. I spend summers with Mum and Jose, which is cool.

I never saw Dad being down about what had happened. The problems only came to the surface later.

And now he must be wondering what's going on. First, he marries Mum and she runs off. Then he gets together with Sharon, they have Flo and now Sharon's making out that he's the worst husband ever.

It's not as if he is, not really.

I reckon it's because he won't talk about stuff. He just keeps a smile on his face and thinks that's enough. I want to help. I want a happy ending.

There was a long pause while I struggled not to let out what I said next. But the words would've choked me if I'd kept them in. 'Dad, maybe you shouldn't go to golf tomorrow morning.'

'Huh? Why not? I always go on Sunday.'

'Yeah, but not tomorrow,' I said again. Then I was stuck. I'd come out with one stupid sentence, and that was it.

Dad laughed. 'What, d'you think I'm gonna get struck by lightning or something?'

I laughed back. 'No. Forget it. I just thought it might be better if you stayed at home, that's all.'

Just in case. Door locks, new keys. Never seeing Flo ever again. I mean, if Rochelle's telling the truth for once . . . But no!

'Don't worry about me, love,' Dad said. Then he wished me luck and said he was proud of me, and he knew I would win first prize.

'Bye, Dad,' I said.

I had to go then, because Rochelle burst into the room with a message for me.

'You have to go down to reception!' Rochelle announced with a weird smile.

'What for?'

Her smile made her look nasty – it was fixed on her face and her eyes were small and mean. Not nice. 'Stacey wants to see you,' she grinned.

I must have looked confused.

'Y'know – Stacey – Stacey Nicholls!'

Right, the *Dreamtime* editor had been at the meal with the other finalists. Maybe she was wondering what had happened to me and how come I hadn't eaten.

'Go!' Roche yelled. 'Now!'

I went.

Nine

I found out there are lots of ways to kill someone's hopes and dreams. You can make them eat a chunk of poisoned apple, or you can choke them on just words.

'Marsha, I have some bad news for you,' Stacey began in a frosty tone.

I thought of a hundred possibilities, but not the right one, as I stood there in reception, with Liberty and Kelly hovering nearby, and Verity chatting to Mrs Walker about the schedule for next day. Stacey didn't bother to keep her voice down, so people picked up right away that something was wrong.

Stacey was different from how I

remembered her. She was still wearing cool clothes, with shorter hair though, and a bit older close to than she looked from a distance. But it was her voice – cool and brisk instead of chatty and honey-sweet.

'We have certain rules of entry for Face of the Year,' she told me, a frown creasing her forehead. 'Basically, you must be thirteen years of age or younger, and you must not have any personal connection with any photographer or member of the panel of judges.'

Out of the corner of my eye I noticed that Verity, the woman who organized us all to be in the right place at the right time, had cut away from Marie's mum to join Stacey and me, and that Rochelle had linked up with Liberty and Kelly in a huddle by the lift.

'I am. I haven't,' I mumbled.

Stacey cut me dead. 'Verity, are we sure that Marsha had a copy of the rules?' she asked.

'Every contestant received them in the same envelope as their entry form,' Verity confirmed stiffly.

A sigh from Stacey told me I was in deep trouble.

'Is there something I should know?' Verity asked, looking confused.

Stacey took her to one side and whispered. This went on a long time, then Verity nodded and she and Stacey came back towards me.

'It's come to my attention that you and Zadie have breached one of the rules,' Verity said. 'And as a result, Marsha, you are disqualified from Face of the Year!'

'I'm twelve!' I said over and over. 'I am. I can prove it!'

Stacey had swept out of the hotel, leaving Verity to shovel me out of sight.

'Come into the office, where we can talk,' Verity suggested, asking the man on reception if we could use his cubby-hole. She obviously didn't want me blubbing in a public place.

'It's not your age that's the problem,' she explained.

The cubby-hole had a table piled high with paper, a hook with a jacket hanging from it. 'I didn't do anything wrong!' I cried.

OK, so I never thought I'd win the contest, but not to be given a chance sucked. I was shaking from head to toe, the inside of my head was a mess.

'Not you. It was Zadie,' Verity said in a voice I could hardly hear.

'Zadie? What did she do?'

'It's difficult . . .'

'No, tell me. What did Zadie do wrong?'

'Oh dear, this is really awkward.' Verity was having a hard time spitting it out. Behind the official clipboard there was a kind woman who didn't want to upset twelve-year-old me. 'I mean, it's tough for Stacey as well as you.'

'What is?' I still wasn't thinking straight, but at least I wasn't blubbing. I just wanted to understand.

Verity sat me down in the one chair in the room. 'Listen, your sister, Zadie, she's – er – she's been seeing – um . . .'

'Domenico!' I gasped.

'Exactly.'

It sank in. 'Y'mean, he's one of the judges?'

Verity nodded. 'A judge as well as a photographer. And he's married to Stacey,' she pointed out. 'Stacey only just found out what's been going on behind her back. Imagine how she must feel.'

I took a deep breath. 'They think that Zadie will persuade Domenico to vote for me?' I asked.

Another nod. 'I'm sorry, Marsha. None of this is down to you, I know.'

'B-but!' I stammered.

'But the rules are very clear, and apparently this little affair has been going on for some time, since well before Zadie entered you for the competition.'

'No, it hasn't!' I yelped. 'She met him at the Riverside. They only went out twice! For a drink – nothing happened!'

'Not according to our information.' Verity was gentle but firm.

'What information? Who told you? Anyhow, they're not seeing each other any more, if they ever really were!' I was spewing stuff dead fast, *rat-a-tat-tat!*

109

Verity tried to smile. 'Nice try, Marsha,' she said coolly.

'It's true!' I felt myself squelching down a slippery mudslide, trying to hang on by my fingernails. OK, so I wouldn't have won, but to go out this way was so unfair!

'You and your sisters have to pack your bags,' Verity insisted. 'We expect you to check out of the hotel first thing in the morning.'

I refused to go quietly. 'Zadie and Dom were never properly going out!' I yelled.

But that didn't get me anywhere. 'You're bound to say that, aren't you?' Verity said, still quiet and considerate, but growing cooler by the second. 'In the circumstances.'

And so I was slipping over the edge, being sucked into a deep hole. 'Who told you?' was my last question before I plunged out of sight.

'Rochelle,' she answered sadly, like she realized my whole family was a mess and she felt sorry for me for being part of it.

Ten

After this, Rochelle acted fast to save her own neck.

I mean, I didn't spot her after I got disqualified. The last time I saw her, she'd been watching the showdown with Stacey, but when I came out of the office with Verity, she was long gone.

Think about it – she'd wrecked my chance of a lifetime and trampled Zadie's name through the mud. No one in their right mind would stick around after that.

'I'll kill her!' Zadie swore, when I told her what had happened. Her face was pale, her hands were shaking. 'Where is she, the little . . . ? Nobody in the fashion photography world is ever gonna take me seriously ever again!' she wailed. 'Domenico will make sure of that. He'll see that every door I knock on is slammed in my face, the louse!'

Noticing that Verity had slipped away, smooth and cool as an ice-cube, I was left to mop up the damage. 'I thought you said Domenico Lane was God,' I muttered bitterly. I couldn't help it – this was as much Zadie's fault as Rochelle's, as far as I was concerned.

Am chucked out of contest. I texted Lisa and Stef.

Zadie stomped around the reception hall for half an hour, then managed to calm down. 'Anyhow, what's so hot about fashion?' she sneered. 'It's just glitz. It doesn't mean anything!'

By this time, the facts were hitting me hard. I was chucked out. It looked like I was a cheat. I'd never be able to face Stef and the kids at school ever again. I sat curled in the chair, staring out of the window at the bright city lights.

'Photo-journalism is what's really hot and happening,' Zadie told herself. 'War zones, terrorist attacks. You have to travel to remote corners, live with the people, wear a flak jacket . . .'

'Puh-lease!' I groaned. I felt wrecked. All I wanted to do was to put my head on the pillow and fall asleep.

But Zadie has no shame. She picked up her phone and texted Jude. **Missing you**, she said.

'Yes, but is it true?' Marie asked me.

I'd spent another sleepless night in the hotel with my bag already packed, hoping that I wouldn't have to face Liberty/Janine/Melody/Kelly over cornflakes and fresh orange juice.

But Zadie wanted to tough it out. 'I don't care what anybody says, we're having breakfast!' she'd declared, dragging me downstairs into the restaurant. She jutted out her chin and went to join the queue for bacon and egg.

This was when Marie sat down beside me

and asked if it was true.

'Yeah, I've been chucked out,' I mumbled, not able to look up and meet her gaze.

'No, I mean – is it true that Zadie and Domenico Lane were an item?'

'Ssh!' I warned. Like, the marmalade jar and the teacups had ears.

'Poor you,' Marie murmured. 'You must feel really grotty.'

I shrugged. 'It saves me losing in front of loads of people, I guess.'

'That's so not true!' Marie frowned. 'D'you say stuff like that just so people will feel sorry for you?'

'No!' I shook my head quickly and glanced up at her.

'OK, so it's because you want them to be nice to you and say, "Don't be stupid, you would've won Face of the Year if you'd had the chance, no contest!" '

'No, definitely not that!' I muttered.

Marie shrugged back at me. 'That's what it sounds like.'

'Right,' I sighed, 'I won't do it again.' And I meant it.

There was a silence then while bacon sizzled behind the breakfast bar.

'Marsha, you're so not tough!' Marie told me after a bit.

I didn't need to hear this. My bag was packed and waiting for me in reception. All I wanted to do was get to King's Cross and hop on that train.

'Yeah well, thanks,' I said with a hollow laugh.

Marie picked up a spoon and tapped it against a cup. 'That's what I mean – you're mega touchy. Here am I trying to help, and there you go, acting like I'm your enemy.'

'Sorry.'

'Don't be. I hear from Janine that it was Rochelle who dropped you and Zadie in it?' *Tap-tap* with the spoon, like she was thinking hard.

I nodded. 'Do you still feel sorry for her?'

'Let's just say I wouldn't want to be inside her head.'

Across the room I could see Zadie loading her plate with saturated fats. 'Well, thanks,' I told Marie, and I was genuine again. *For talking to me when you needn't have, for being a good friend even though I've only known you for two days.* I didn't say that bit, of course.

'So is it – true?'

Zadie came towards us, balancing her plate, trying to tough it out but actually looking as if she wished we'd skipped breakfast after all. She slid past Verity, who sat chatting with Marie's mum.

And for the first time, Marie's question sank in. Was it true that Domenico and Zadie had really been an item? I stared at my stepsister and remembered her singing about Kansas corn and American flags.

'Well, she definitely fancied him,' I sighed.

She'd been out for a meal with him, he'd looked at her portfolio, ha-ha!

But then I thought again. Hadn't I been up in the pod with Dom? Hadn't he warned me to stop Zadie coming on strong?

I tried to picture their conversation and think this is probably how it had gone:

Dom: Look, I don't want, have never wanted, will never want to go out with you, OK!

Zadie: B-b-but!

Dom: Read my lips! I don't mind talking about photography and lapping up your flattery, but that's all there is to it!

Zadie: You're not serious!

Dom: I'm married. Be a good girl and leave me alone.

And, 'Wow!' I gasped now, as Zadie sat down at the table with her bacon. 'I don't know if any of it's true! Zadie, give it to us straight – did you and Dom, I mean – were you – did you ever – or was it . . .?'

Marie jumped in and rescued me. 'Were you and Dom ever actually dating, Zadie?' she asked in her up-front, sing-song voice. 'Or was your friendship with him purely platonic?'

You really need the dictionary for this one, believe me.

platonic *or* **Platonic** (say *pla-tonnik*) *adjective*
spiritual as distinct from sexual or sensual:
'*platonic* love'
Word family: **platonically** *adverb*
[after *Plato*, an ancient Greek philosopher who advocated ideal love]

* * *

I could go and get on that train now, I thought. There was nothing to stop me. No Face of the Year, no brilliant future alongside Mary-Kate-and-Ashley. No, I could zap up home and stop Sharon changing the locks, ha-ha.

And yet, as I sat and watched the light dawn in Zadie's eyes, I knew I wouldn't.

'That's it!' she cried.

'That's what?' I asked.

Marie nodded and asked Zadie to say more, encouraging her to come clean in front of Verity, Marie's mum and the rest.

'That's it – my relationship with Domenico Lane was professional. I admire him; one photographer to another. I asked his advice and he gave it. End of story!'

'So you weren't an item?' Marie double-checked.

Zadie sighed in a don't-be-stupid style. 'No way. Is that what they're saying?'

'You *know* that's what they're saying!' I hissed, not realizing that Zadie was playing to an audience.

There were four other Face of the Year contestants, plus Mrs Walker and Verity in the restaurant, remember.

Zadie gave a little laugh, loud enough to draw attention. 'Domenico Lane is a cool guy,' she admitted. 'As a photographer, he's in the premier league. But hey, he's way too old for me!'

I heard Janine gasp and saw her whisper across her table to Melody. Verity picked up her mobile phone and looked like she might punch a text message into it.

'Are you denying that you were Dom's girlfriend?' Marie asked in a stunned voice. Her acting was as good as Zadie's. If she doesn't make it as a model, she'll definitely have a place in the movies. 'Isn't it true that you and he were dating long before you sent in Marsha's picture for the competition?'

'No way!' Zadie told her. 'I didn't even know he was one of the judges!'

True. I swear.

'And you saw him as a kind of hero in the fashion photography world?' Marie went on. If not an actress, I think she should be a solicitor when she leaves school. The first supermodel with a law degree. 'Someone whose advice you wanted to ask?'

Zadie nodded. 'But that's all. I swear!'

'Swear?'

'Yeah!'

By this time, I was feeling a bit queasy, remembering Zadie singing in the shower. 'Never mind. Let's just leave it,' I hissed at Marie.

'But you know what this means?' she frowned. 'Marsha, they've chucked you out without any reason!'

By this time Verity was standing up and asking if anyone had seen Stacey. The whole room was buzzing, Melody and Janine were looking daggers at our table.

'It's not fair!' Marie objected. 'I don't know how this rumour about Dom and Zadie got around, but at least somebody could have checked it out before they started chucking Marsha off the contest!'

I stood up now, then sat down again with a bump. Which shows how much in two minds I was. Run for the train, or stay and fight to get back into Face of the Year?

'Yes!' Zadie agreed with Marie. 'They never even gave me a chance to deny it!'

'Or Dom,' Marie pointed out.

Wow, was she good!

'Did anyone think to ask him?'

There was panic on Verity's face as events ran out of control.

Zadie pushed away her plate of globby bacon. 'No!' she declared. 'I don't suppose anybody asked *Dom* whether or not we'd been having an affair!'

Verity clamped her phone to her ear and ran from the room.

'How about doing it now?' Marie wanted to know.

Zadie took a deep breath and hauled me to my feet. 'Let's go!' she said, holding me in an iron grip.

Eleven

So, no train and no chance to stop Dad going to golf.

By now Rochelle would be with her mum, laughing with Sharon about me being disqualified. If she'd been telling me the truth, they'd soon be visiting the DIY store, buying new door locks.

'You're mad!' I said to Marie as we all dashed to Tussauds in a taxi.

Zadie rehearsed the speech she was going to make to Dom. 'Tell your wife that you and I never met before the Riverside, and yes we may have got together to discuss my college course and my work, but that was it! There was never anything except business between us!'

She tried this in several different voices, from weak and pleading to loud and bossy.

'Whatever you do, stay calm,' was Mrs Walker's advice, but she didn't know Zadie like I do.

My phone buzzed and received a text. When I took it out and looked at it, there were two unread messages.

The one from Lisa said, **What do u mean, chucked out?**

Dad's said, **Good luck!**

The taxi dropped us on Marylebone Road, outside the waxworks, with Zadie in fighting mood. 'If it's a showdown he wants, that's what he's gonna get!' she promised, striding out across the pavement.

Mrs Walker cleared her throat. 'Best take it easy,' she advised, backpedalling like mad. 'After all, we don't want to make things worse.'

Zadie paused under a giant poster showing the Chamber of Horrors. There was a dark dungeon with chains hanging from the slimy wall. *'Think you can handle the Chamber?'* it read. *'There's no escape. Are you brave enough to come out the other side with a smile on your face?'*

'This is my reputation we're talking about,' Zadie insisted. 'I have to clear my name!'

'Yes, and get Marsha back into the contest,' Marie reminded her.

We marched to the head of the queue, flashed our *Dreamtime* badges and went through the barrier.

'How do we know that Dom will be here?' I asked, though a glance at my watch told me that it was just over an hour before the start of the morning's shooting, and if he wasn't here now, he soon would be.

We followed Face of the Year signs down a corridor until we came to the team of stylists at work on the five other kids, and Mrs Walker hustled Marie off to join them. They were on the edge of an area called Premiere Night, where the morning's shoot was set to take place.

'Hope this works out!' Marie whispered to me, before the hairdresser pounced.

'Thanks!' I said, then ducked out of sight and joined Zadie in Sporting Legends.

We were rubbing shoulders with David Beckham when I first got the chance to seriously discuss with Zadie what we were trying to do.

It's weird – the models look dead lifelike, but their skin is made of wax, like candles. They measure the real person in hundreds of places, then make a mould and pour the wax in. They even copy the designer stubble.

'Is this gonna work?' I asked Zadie over David's shoulder. He was in his shaved head phase, in an England shirt.

'It will if we can find Dom,' she said through gritted teeth.

'Yes, but will it work in time?' I reckoned we only had half an hour max to get to him in Premiere Night and make him deny the affair. After that, Stacey and the judges would have gathered and the shoot would begin without me.

'I'm gonna kill Rochelle!' Zadie said for

about the fiftieth time, bumping into Andre Agassi.

I sidestepped Muhammad Ali. 'Marie's cool,' I pointed out, to change the subject.

Zadie agreed. 'You still need to beat her, though.'

'I do?'

'Yeah, in the competition, when they let you back in.'

'*If!*' I insisted. '*If* they let me back in!'

'The thing is, if they see us, they'll throw us out,' Zadie reminded me. 'We're not even supposed to be here.'

'Yeah, so we can hardly walk up to Verity and ask where Dom is, can we?'

'No, we have to be sneaky.'

No problem there, then. Zadie does sneaky nearly as well as Rochelle.

'And fast,' I added, letting my panic show. Serena Williams crouched low, ready to receive serve.

'OK then, let's sneak!' Zadie hissed, approaching the guy on the door of Premiere Night. 'I'm with one of the kids in the contest,' she said, giving him a flirty smile.

'Her name's Marie Walker. Sorry, I lost my badge!'

The bouncer checked names on a list and decided to let Zadie through. But when he saw me walking up to him, he put on his big, bad voice. 'You can't come in here,' he barked.

I panicked. 'I'm a contestant,' I mumbled. 'My name's Marsha Martinez.'

Doh! A disqualified contestant, if you did but know. I was mad at myself for not thinking on my feet.

Bouncy Man checked the list again and nodded me through.

Yeah! It seems Verity had slipped up and forgotten to have my name crossed off. So I nipped in and tried to lose myself in the crowd of photographers, stylists and competitors' relatives crammed into the small, cordoned-off area beside Premiere Night.

But then it looked like Ms Clipboard had made another mistake, because a stylist grabbed me and nearly yanked my arm off as she pulled me to a seat by a mirror. In other words, here was another person who didn't know I'd been chucked out.

'God, Marsha, we thought you'd got lost!' she complained, clapping a plastic shawl around my shoulders, slapping on the foundation and beginning the magic transformation. 'What kept you?'

'I was – we were looking for someone,' I told her.

'Has anyone seen Stacey?' a man's voice asked from the other side of the mirror. 'Verity needs to speak to her, but Stacey's phone is switched off!'

'No, sorry, I haven't seen her!' came the answer.

The stylist blushered me with a brush the size of a fist. She slicked on the lip-gloss then thickened and curled my eyelashes. When she'd made me over, she tipped me out of the chair. 'Go see Meera in wardrobe,' she ordered. 'Last I heard she was threatening to give your outfit to Janine unless you showed up double quick.'

'Where's Stacey? Has anyone seen her?' This time it was Verity herself who came blundering through the crowd.

I hid behind a screen advertising Sporting Legends until she'd passed. Which was when I spotted Dom, by himself, quietly setting up lights inside the Premiere Night space.

This was my chance. Obviously. I mean, it must have been fate.

For a few seconds I watched him tilt spotlights and trail wires across the floor, trying to force myself to sneak over and talk to him.

He's busy. He won't want to listen, I dithered.

Then I thought of Rochelle, and the way she'd turned my dream chance into a living nightmare, and from somewhere I found the guts to step out from behind the screen and make my way towards Mr Fashion Photography.

He was crouched in a dark corner next to a wall socket with his back towards me when I said my first sentence.

'Could you do me a favour?'

He swivelled round to face me. 'Sorry?'

'I'm Marsha Martinez. Zadie's sister.' Whoa, my heart was thumping like crazy. My mouth was dry.

'Yep?'

Dom looked tired. He had dark rings under his eyes and thick stubble on his chin. I thought maybe Stacey had rowed with him and chucked him out because of Zadie. He definitely hadn't had much sleep.

'I want you to get me back into the contest,' I said quietly. *Thump-thump*, like a hammer inside my chest. 'You can if you tell Stacey that you and Zadie didn't really go out together.'

Dom went from a squat to a sit and leaned his back against the wall. 'Just run that by me again,' he said wearily.

'You have to tell Stacey that you and Zadie weren't an item,' I insisted. 'Then they'll let me back into the final.'

Slowly he took this in. 'Right. You want me to go to my wife, who by the way isn't speaking to me any more, and rake up this whole mess again, just so you can swan down a catwalk for thirty seconds?'

Put like that, it didn't sound like something he would be willing to do for me.

'Yes,' I said faintly.

He tilted his head back against the wall and looked at me through slitted eyes. 'I've kind of done that a million times already,' he muttered. 'Like, "Stacey, honey, I never even laid a finger on the girl, I swear to God!" The thing is, she doesn't believe me.'

'Oh!' This was bad news – an angle which Marie hadn't thought of. 'Couldn't you tell her again?'

Dom shook his head. 'Sorry, I'm out of credit.'

'Meaning?'

'She won't listen. She's had it with my "floozies", as she calls them.' Running a hand through his non-existent hair, Dom hauled himself to his feet. 'You wanna know something funny?' he asked.

'What?' Behind me I could hear Verity calling the kids' names in the order they would appear. Spotlights were being switched on. Jennifer Aniston and Brad Pitt smiled their waxwork smiles.

'Your sister, Zadie – she flung herself at me.'

'Yeah,' I nodded. *She would*.

'And for once in my life I resisted,' Dom said with a weak grin. 'I said no way, and yet still I get the flak. How crazy is that?'

'Mad,' I sighed. 'So you won't talk to Stacey for me? Not even if I tell you that it was my other sister, Rochelle, who's jealous, so she blew this whole thing up into a major crisis and lied to your wife?'

'Where's Dom?' Verity was calling across the room while we stayed tucked out of the way in the dark corner. 'We're ready to shoot!'

'Hey, with sisters like that, who needs enemies?' Dom half-laughed, though we both knew it wasn't funny. 'Any idea why Rochelle would do that to you?'

'Yeah.' But I didn't have time to go into it with him.

He looked hard at me, then stooped to flick the socket switch. 'I'm sorry, kid,' he muttered. 'But there ain't a thing I can do.'

* * *

The room was laid out like the entrance to a film premiere. There was a big cinema doorway, with a red carpet stretching across a fake pavement into the foyer, and on the carpet the stars posed.

There was Jennifer and Brad, Keanu and Russell, with James Bond and Harry Potter hovering by the glitzy entrance.

The thing was that each kid in the final got to walk the red carpet. The photographers would take pictures as she schmoozed with the 'stars'. The judges would watch, discuss and choose the winner.

'Ready!' Verity called, clipboard in hand.

No, not ready. I'm in the dark, on the outside. I've come all this way, gone through all this, only to be chucked out. Unless . . .

Liberty was the first on the carpet, in sparkly denim crop top and white trousers. She'd practised her movie star walk, shoulders back, flicking her long blonde hair behind her. When she stopped to link arms with Harry P and share his long scarf, Dom and the other photographers clicked like crazy.

Unless ... I try something here. It's gonna make my heart thump again and my palms go sweaty. I'm gonna have to look cool, even though I don't feel it ...

Janine went next, dressed in an outfit consisting of a black crop top and drawstring trousers. She slid in between Jennifer and Brad with a cheesy grin.

'What happened to you?' Meera asked me when I sprinted into the wardrobe department. There was one set of clothes left on a hanger, waiting for me to wear them.

'I got held up in make-up,' I told her, stripping down to my undies.

'These were supposed to be for Janine, but she liked your outfit better and I thought you'd chickened out.' Meera handed me a matching ra-ra skirt and halter top in lilac satin (definitely not my style), with a loose silver belt to drape around my hips and a funky, chunky silver necklace (more my thing). My shoes were cream, knee-high suede boots.

'Check that out!' Meera said, pointing me towards the mirror.

I didn't have time to look at my lilac satin self for long though, because a kid called Amy, who I haven't mentioned before, was strutting the red carpet, number four after Liberty, Janine and Marie.

'What about your hair?' Meera called after me as I dashed to stand in line behind Melody and Kelly.

I glanced at it and saw it was mussed up like I hadn't combed it since I got out of bed. 'It's meant to look like this!' I lied.

So far, no one had stopped me, fingers crossed. I was at the back of the queue, music was blaring out, cameras were flashing.

'OK, Melody, do your stuff!' Verity said, sending finalist number five on to the red carpet.

That was when she spotted me in my lilac gear and almost dropped her clipboard. 'Marsha?'

Boom-boom-boom. My ribs took a real

beating. 'You heard what Zadie said earlier – she never went out with Dom!' I reminded her, holding my head high. It was one of those moments when you think, what the heck! If you have enough nerve, it might just carry you through.

'We disqualified you!' Verity hissed, one eye on Melody posing with Pierce Brosnan, one eye on me. She stood right across my path like a sentry on parade. 'I haven't had a chance to talk to Stacey. She's gonna go ballistic if she sees you!'

Kelly – one of the ones with the most modelling experience – gave me the dead eye. *Yeah, they chucked you out!*

'But Rochelle was lying! You never gave us a chance to prove it. Ask Zadie. Ask Dom!'

'No time,' Verity told me, bundling Kelly on to the carpet.

'Please!' I said. 'I deserve this!'

She stared at me, the corners of her eyes screwed up into tiny wrinkles. Then she took a deep breath, and without saying anything, she stepped to one side.

* * *

I was last of the seven along the red carpet. Jennifer smiled at me; there was a twinkle in Brad's glass eye.

My satin frills swished as I walked, my bling blinged in the flash of camera lights.

Hi, Keanu, hey there, Harry! I twirled and strutted my stuff among the stars.

I came off the red carpet and the music stopped. Silence.

After the flashing cameras, it took ages for my eyes to get used to the normal light.

'Cool!' Marie told me. 'The girl did real good!'

'I thought she'd been chucked out!' Melody whispered to Kelly. 'Why didn't Verity stop her?'

All this was a blur of faces and low sounds. I was breathing fast. Was I in or out of the contest? Did I stand any chance of being Face of the Year?

'Marsha!'

I heard my name. I looked round, still not seeing clearly.

'Marsha!' Verity said again. She was calling from a distance, where the knot of photographers and judges had got their heads together to discuss their verdict.

OK, so it hadn't worked out. Maybe I hadn't even expected it to. But at least I'd got out there with the other six kids. No one would ever know how much nerve that had taken.

Hearing my name a third time, I dragged myself towards Verity to be given the bad news.

'Someone's here to see you,' she told me.

Not, 'Sorry, Marsha. Stacey says no way.'

I looked up and saw the last person I would've expected.

'Dad!' I gasped. 'What're you doing here?'

Twelve

My dad at a fashion shoot is definitely a total fish out of water.

'How? What? Why?' I muttered. Like, *Dad, how did you get here? What the heck made you drive all the way down? Why aren't you at home saving your marriage?*

He stood there in his yellow golfing sweater and baggy beige trousers, hands shoved deep in his pockets. 'Hi, Marsh. Did you win?'

'Ssh!' I hissed, taking a nervous sideways glance at Verity. 'The judges are still making up their minds.'

Verity looked down at her clipboard, muttered something which might have been,

'I'll have another word with Stacey,' then walked away.

'Dad,' I said again. 'What are you doing here?'

Remember, this was going on in the middle of a room full of glam girlies and their twittering mums. We were squashed between the stylists and the waxworks, melting under bright spotlights, pinned against the wall by Jennifer and Brad.

'Aren't you pleased I came?' Dad grinned. 'Say yes – I had to set off at six this morning!'

'No!' I cried. 'Just answer the question, Dad!'

He shrugged. 'I thought you sounded a bit off on the phone yesterday.'

'That's so not true!' I protested. 'I was fine, honest!'

'I know you said you were fine, but you didn't sound it.'

I stared at him. Suddenly my bright-and-cheery-everything's-OK dad had turned into a New Man – the sensitive sort who picks up the signals when you're not feeling yourself and comes to give you

a big hug to make you better. 'Wow!'
I said.

'Don't look at me like that. I was right,
wasn't I?'

I squirmed and looked down at my fawn
suede boots. Don't mention the door locks,
or Dad cheating on Sharon, and never seeing
Flo again. That's stuff he does *not* need to
know! 'Rochelle had been mean to me, that's
all.'

'Hmm.' Dad's hands came out of his
pockets and he folded his arms. 'Spoiling
your party, was she?'

'Something like that. So what's new?'

For a little while I let Dad chew on
this and switched to Stacey and the other
judges, who were studying pictures of
the contestants, trying to make up their
minds.

Was I in or out? I still didn't know. Six
other kids and their mums were asking, *Is it
me? Please, please, let it be me!*

Then Zadie popped up. 'You little star!'
she grinned, hugging me and nearly
squeezing me to death. 'I didn't think you

had the guts to ignore everything and just get up there and do that!'

'Ignore what?' Dad asked. 'What's going on here?'

Verity leaned over Stacey's shoulder and whispered. Stacey glanced over the table at Dom, then across the room at me.

Was I in? Or out?

'Nothing,' I muttered to Dad.

'Rochelle only went and got Marsha chucked out of the competition!' Zadie declared, conveniently forgetting the part she'd played. 'She made up a stupid story about us cheating.'

Dad's eyebrows shot up. 'Why didn't you tell me, Marsh?'

' 'Cos it hadn't happened when I spoke to you.'

'Right.' He thought hard for a bit. 'But you didn't cheat, so they let you back in,' he checked. 'I've just seen you doing your stuff.'

It was my turn to shrug. 'Dunno yet.'

'We're gonna kill Rochelle!' Zadie promised. 'I bet she didn't say anything to you when she got back!'

Poor Dad's eyebrows were shooting about all over the place. Right now they were pulled together in a tight frown. 'You're saying Rochelle came home early?'

Zadie nodded. 'Yeah. Why?'

'She didn't – that's why.'

I was looking from one to the other like a spectator at a tennis match.

'Well, she took off from the hotel last night,' Zadie told him. 'She knew not to stick around after what she'd done!'

'Hold it!' Dad needed to think. 'If Rochelle didn't come home to Wentworth Road, she must've gone to stay with Sharon at Helen's. Only, I can't call and check that out, 'cos Sharon's still not answering her phone.'

I sighed. This was all we needed.

'I'll do it,' Zadie offered, taking out her phone but not getting a strong enough signal. 'Later,' she added.

'Do it now!' Dad insisted.

So Zadie went outside to make the call.

'This is all you need,' Dad said, reading my thoughts. Telepathic Dad.

Him being kind made the tears well up. I

fought to hold them back, but it's weird – the more you try the harder it is to stop them.

'Don't cry, kid,' Dad murmured. 'See, the judges are ready to announce the winner.'

I made myself watch and saw that Stacey had stood up to make an announcement. She was smiling, looking good in a floaty white top with a bright orange and blue swirly pattern. The other judges and photographers were grouped around her.

'Hi, everyone,' she began, 'and especially hi and thanks for entering our competition to a group of fab gals with bags and bags of talent!'

Seven of us blushed and gave modest grins, even if in secret we would've scrambled over each other's dead bodies to be Face of the Year. Melody and Janine stood near the front, and I could make out Amy with her mum, plus Marie a little bit to the front of me. She turned and gave me a quick smile.

Just to remind you – I've got tears rolling down my cheeks, my dad standing next to me, a missing stepsister, a stepmum who's gone off her trolley, and I don't even know if I'm included in the group of fab gals.

'I know you're all here hoping that your dream will come true,' Stacey went on. 'And yes it's corny, but we wish we could make it happen for every single one of you.'

There was a pause and total silence in the room.

When Stacey began again, the smile had gone and her voice was serious. 'Before I go on to announce our Face of the Year, I want to mention one person here who has had a pretty bumpy ride in the last twenty-four hours.'

Another pause. It was only because Marie turned again and looked at me that I realized that Stacey meant me.

'Marsha Martinez is one of our northern finalists, and since yesterday there's been doubt about whether or not she qualified for the competition.'

Everyone turned to stare. I froze. Dad put his arm around my shoulder.

'Like I say, it hasn't been easy,' Stacey said.

Was I in? Was I? Or was this the moment when I crawled under a stone?

'But we, the judges and the administrator, Verity Jones, have put our heads together to discuss the problem, and we've decided, according to fresh evidence, that Marsha didn't break the rules after all.'

I'm in! I made it! Wowee-zowie!

Dad gives me a hug.

Now I feel I can do anything. Chuck any problem at me and I'll solve it. Ask me to fly to the moon!

Next to Stacey, Dom and Verity are smiling in my direction. I know they've spoken up for me and helped me get back into the contest. Thanks, Verity. And Dom isn't all bad either, though he's still a rat mostly.

But have I won Face of the Year?

'So we've been considering all seven finalists,' Stacey told us. 'But as you know, only one of you can be *Dreamtime*'s cover gal . . .'

Please get a move on, put us out of our misery!

Every pair of eyes in the room is fixed on

Stacey. I don't turn around when Zadie comes up beside me to listen to the result.

'Our Face of the Year has to be fresh and natural. Our model has to say "Life is Fun!" '

Jeez, I wish I'd smiled more!

'At the same time, she has to be interesting and a little bit different.'

OK, so maybe the stroppy look isn't a total no-no.

'I'll say again, you all have what it takes, and you all have a look that's right for now.' Stacey spun it out, like they do on *Pop Idol*.

'But!' she said finally, 'we have chosen someone who for us stands out above all the rest for sheer pazazz. And the winner of *Dreamtime* Face of the Year is ... Janine Young!'

Thirteen

Janine Young!

Yeah, you can feel the disappointment, like a music tape stretching and the notes going all whiny. *Da-da-dah-duuurrrgh!*

I mean, I know what you're thinking – if I hadn't won, it could at least have been Marie.

Janine jumped about in my black crop top and drawstring trousers. She squealed and clasped her hands to her mouth. Her mum hugged her. We glam girlies all put on fake smiles and clapped. Janine has tousled blonde hair parted to one side and draped over her big blue eyes. Watch out Mary-Kate-and-Ashley.

I'll try to be nicer about people in future, I promise.

'Hard luck, Marsh,' Dad said.

I swallowed the lump in my throat and smiled back.

Marie came up and gave me her e-mail address and phone number. 'Come and see me in Stirling some time, but don't bring Rochelle,' she grinned.

I texted Lisa – **They let me back in. Didn't win**.

I was just getting over the disappointment when Dad gave a little cough to warn me that Stacey Nicholls, Domenico Lane and the woman from the Choice Model Agency were heading our way.

Stacey shook Dad's hand. 'Are you OK?' she asked me, maybe noticing my smudgy panda eyes.

I nodded. Back to my usual talkative self.

'You were so right to hang on in there,' Stacey said. 'And I'm sorry I gave you such a hard time. The trouble was, I flew off the handle when I first heard the silly story about Dom and Zadie.'

This was the point when Stacey turned to my stepsister. Her voice was light and fake-friendly – the type women use when they want to put you down. 'Now, Zadie, I know the truth, and of course I can appreciate that Dom is exactly the person you would choose to ask advice about a career in photography, so I don't blame you at all for any of this mess.'

Zadie went bright red and shuffled her feet.

'And Dom is mega generous with his time as far as students go,' Stacey smiled, turning back to me.

Dom said nothing.

('He is *so* under the thumb!' Zadie said later. I said I thought he was *so* not in a position to argue!)

'Marsha, you did really well. We admire your guts, and Melanie, for one, wants you on her pre-teen list.'

I gulped. 'Really?'

Melanie Duchamp said yes, she was pretty sure she could find me some magazine work. 'I like your look,' she told me. 'Get

Zadie to build up a portfolio for you and send it to me. We'll take it from there.'

So I did get something out of the contest, even though I might not be Face of the Year.

And, for sure I got a lot more than I expected when Zadie took that first stroppy photo with her Fuji Finepix.

I was behind a screen, getting changed out of my satin frills into my jeans and trainers, when Zadie came to find me.

'I've got something to tell you,' she muttered in a worried voice.

I Velcroed my shoes and stood up. 'Sharon wants a divorce,' I guessed, only half joking. At the back of my head I still had the idea that Rochelle hadn't just been winding me up about the door locks.

Zadie shook her head. 'I'm serious.'

'Me too.' Here was Dad at Madame Tussauds, looking after me, and there was my stepmum busy locking us out.

'Listen, that's up to Mum and Tony – it's their stuff. No, this is something else.'

I guessed again. 'About Rochelle?'

This time she nodded. 'I spoke to Mum, and she says Roche didn't go back to Helen's last night.'

'So where did she go?'

Zadie took a deep breath. 'That's just it. We don't know!'

I wasn't feeling anything, and then suddenly, out of the blue, I cared. I thought of Rochelle legging it out of the hotel, getting lost in the Underground and then what . . . ? You know me – give me a crisis and I think the worst.

'Roche has vanished!' Zadie said, dragging me through the celebs to find Dad.

'OK, so did she have her train ticket with her?' was Dad's first question.

He didn't panic, but I could see he was worried.

Zadie nodded. 'She bought hers separately from Marsha and me. Is there any way we can find out if she used it?'

Dad shook his head. 'It's not like a plane, where they check you in. So where does that leave us? We know she realized she was in trouble.'

'Yeah, I'll kill her!' Zadie said, but in a wobbly voice.

'She was in reception when Stacey chucked me out,' I confirmed. 'Last I saw, Roche was having a laugh about it with two other kids.'

'So what did she do after that?' Dad wondered. 'Zadie, help us out here – you know her better than anyone else.'

Zadie thought for a while. 'She's a complicated kid, and I think she'd get a buzz out of what she'd done, but at the same time she'd be feeling a little bit guilty.'

Complicated? Guilty? Was this the same Rochelle we were talking about?

'How guilty?' Dad asked.

'Enough to make her leg it,' Zadie said. 'Trouble is, she's tough, but she doesn't know London.'

We were stuck then, standing on a busy pavement on Marylebone Road.

'How did Sharon react when you called her?' Dad asked.

Zadie rolled her eyes. 'You don't wanna know. Let's just say, she wasn't a happy bunny.'

I was breathing in exhaust fumes from a double-decker bus when I had a brainwave. 'Let's call her!'

So we tried on Zadie's phone, but she got the machine voice telling her Roche was unavailable. 'She's switched off,' Zadie muttered.

'Maybe I should ring Sharon,' Dad sighed.

'No way!' Zadie insisted.

Then my phone rang, and talk of the devil, it was Sharon.

Sharon: Marsha, where's Rochelle?

Me: I dunno.

Sharon: Of course you know!

Me: I don't.

Sharon: What did you say to her? Why did she leave the hotel?

Me: I didn't say anything. It was her.

Sharon: (in a high-pitched voice) I knew it! You two have argued. You upset her – that's why she ran off!

Me: Me? *I* upset *her*!

Sharon: Marsha, why can't you leave Rochelle alone? You're always getting at her and making her life a misery. And now look!

Me: Here's Dad (*handing over the phone as if it's red hot*).

Dad: Sharon, it's me.

Silence.

Dad: Sharon?

Silence.

'She rang off,' Dad said in a flat voice, handing my phone back to me.

'Let's go back to the hotel,' Zadie suggested. 'Maybe Rochelle told someone there what she planned to do.'

There was a new receptionist on duty who didn't have a clue who Rochelle was or why we were worried about her.

'Sorry, all I know is that the room you were in is now booked to a Mr and Mrs Jennings,' she said, clicking a few buttons and peering at a computer screen.

'Where's the guy who was on duty yesterday?' Zadie wanted to know.

'*Off* duty,' Ms Snooty said, looking down her nose.

Dad took charge. 'We'd like to speak to the manager, please.'

Snooty Boots sighed. Two people came to the desk to check out, so she dealt with them instead.

Then Verity came out of the lift carrying her suitcase. She smiled when she saw me. 'Good job, Marsha. I hope things work out for you with the Choice Agency.'

'Thanks,' I smiled back. 'And thanks – for, you know . . .'

'Listen, get me the manager,' Dad was saying to the receptionist.

'Problem?' Verity asked helpfully. 'If it's the bill, it's been paid by *Dreamtime*.'

'No, it's not that. It's Rochelle. We thought she'd gone home last night, but she didn't.'

'Huh.' Verity scrunched up her mouth and eyes as if she was trying to remember something. 'Wait here a sec,' she said, putting down her bag and hurrying off towards the restaurant.

She came back with the waiter who'd

served us on the first night we were there. 'Talk to Tom,' she told us. 'He might be able to help.'

Tom, the crème brûlée waiter, looked like he'd just been arrested. The corners of his mouth were turned down in a 'wot me, gov?' expression. He wasn't much more than sixteen, with short fair hair and grey eyes. 'You looking for Rochelle?' he mumbled.

We nodded.

'I gave her a lift,' he told us in an Irish accent. 'She asked me how to get to King's Cross. I was going off duty, so I took her there.'

'I saw them leaving together,' Verity confirmed.

Dad nodded. 'You took her all the way to the station?' he asked the kid.

'Yeah. The next train wasn't due for forty minutes, so we went for a coffee.'

'How did she seem?' Dad pushed for more information. 'Was she upset?'

Tom shook his head. 'Not exactly. She could hardly wait to get on that train though – y'know, kind of jumpy.'

'Well, that was nice of you to help, thanks.'

' 'S cool, no problem.'

'She didn't tell you where she was heading, by any chance?' Zadie asked. The Irish waiter was way too young for her, but he looked like Ronan Keating, so she still came on to him with the big eyes.

Tom shrugged. 'Home?'

'No,' Zadie said. 'That's the problem.'

Her phone rang, and it was – you guessed it – Sharon again. 'Yeah, hi, Mum,' Zadie said. 'No, we haven't found her . . . Yes, we know she got on the train . . . No, just try to stay calm, will you? . . . Yeah, there was a problem with the competition . . . No, it wasn't Marsha's fault . . . Listen, Mum!'

I didn't want to hear any more, so I walked off, quickly followed by Dad.

'Jump in the car,' he ordered. 'We're heading north and we've got a long drive ahead of us.'

Fourteen

Long drive, as in five and a half hours because of the traffic.

Sunday afternoon is when everyone heads home from a weekend away, snarling up the M25 around Heathrow and choking the M1 in both directions. No one said much for the first hundred miles.

Then Zadie had a text from Jude which read, **Manchstr sucks without u**, so that put a thoughtful smile back on her face.

Miss u 2, she texted back after a while. 'I really do,' she told me. 'Jude and I go back a long way. Trouble is, I take him for granted.'

'Yeah,' I nodded.

'OK, so I was out of order,' Zadie admitted. 'I won't do it again.'

'Yeah. No.'

'I wish I knew what all this was about,' Dad sighed, tapping the steering wheel and staring ahead at the slow crawl of traffic up the hill towards Nottingham.

I explained again about Rochelle getting me chucked out of the contest.

'No, I mean, what this is really about,' he insisted. 'Why don't you two get on?'

I was in the back seat, gawping at him in the overhead mirror. He saw my reflection. 'Close your mouth, Marsh, and talk to me.'

This was the man who grinned his way through everything and would refuse to admit there was a problem even if his house had been torn apart by a hurricane.

'I can tell you what's wrong with Rochelle,' Zadie volunteered. 'I mean, it's blindingly obvious – Marsh is prettier than her, end of story.'

Press the Pause button, Rewind, Play.

* * *

'Marsh is prettier than her, end of story.'

I didn't believe Zadie had just said that. My chin practically hit the floor.

'She's jealous,' Zadie went on. 'Y'know, mirror, mirror, on the wall ... Roche has tried everything she knows to get the right answer, including putting in blonde streaks, and slapping on the foundation an inch thick, but the mirror still tells her that Marsh has got it and she hasn't.'

'She has!' I argued. 'Roche is dead pretty!'

Help! Did I just say that?

'She doesn't think she is,' Zadie insisted. 'Believe me, Roche is really insecure about the way she looks.'

'Blimey,' Dad said. 'Show me the bloke who understands women, and I'll give you a million quid.'

We went another fifty miles without talking. Radio 1 blasted out the Top Twenty.

'Y'know, when you think about it, it all makes sense,' Dad decided halfway over the Sheffield viaduct, squashed between a lorry and an Audi TT.

'It does?' Zadie muttered, looking over her shoulder at me, as if to say, *What's got into him?*

'Yep. Rochelle feels threatened by Marsh – that's why she's always looking for a fight.'

I rolled my eyes and sighed. 'So it's still my fault?'

'No, 'course not. You haven't done anything wrong. But it can't have been easy for Roche when Shaz and I got together, and unluckily for you, Marsh, Roche took it all out on you. The same with Shaz – when she sees Roche going off the rails, she looks around for someone to blame, and who does she choose?'

'Me!' I groaned, followed by, 'Sorry I exist!'

Dad went on working it all out. 'I wish I'd spotted it earlier, but I just went along expecting everyone to get on, and tough luck if they didn't. And of course, Shaz had a hard time when Flo was born, which didn't help.'

Zadie and I were staring at him wide eyed. 'You should consider going to work for Relate,' Zadie told him.

Dad laughed self-consciously. 'I'm an idiot.'

Silence from us. This is where I could've jumped in and told him how much of an idiot he was to trust Sharon, who had just walked out on him and taken Flo with her. Plus the fact that she thought he was having an affair and was going to lock him out of his own house. Only this wasn't a fact exactly, it was Rochelle's version of the truth.

I chewed my lip on the back seat as the DJ reached the Number One slot. We came into Leeds city centre, out by the university, heading for home.

Wentworth Road is an ordinary street of semis with cars parked in the drives because the garages are full of junk. It's a no-through road, and kids skateboard on the concrete ramp leading into a little office complex at the far end, which drives Sharon mad.

It was nearly seven o'clock when Dad pulled up outside our house.

'Let's get inside and dump your stuff,' Dad suggested to Zadie and me. 'Then we've got to do some serious thinking about tracking down Rochelle.'

He made it sound easy, but to me there was a giant question mark even over the 'let's get inside' bit.

'I hope that kid realizes what she's doing to this family!' Zadie muttered as she followed Dad up the path.

This family. The Hoddles and the Martinezes. *United we stand!*

I held my breath as he took his key out of his pocket and slid it into the lock.

'Please turn!' I prayed.

Dad twisted the key. It jammed.

My heart dropped like a stone into my trainers.

'Wrong key,' Dad grunted, trying again. This time the key clicked and unlocked the door.

I started to breathe again. My next thought was the original, 'I'm gonna kill Rochelle!', and the next was, '*If* we ever find her!'

I've never felt so relieved, just being able to walk in through my own front door!

'That's funny!' Dad said, checking the

central heating control. 'I'm sure I switched that off.'

Zadie dumped her bag in the hallway, while I wandered into the kitchen. The light was on. There was baby food on the table and Flo sitting in her high chair.

'Oog!' she said, jamming her podgy fist into her mouth.

'Dad!' I yelled.

It's only afterwards that you realize how wound up you were.

First of all there was the relief of seeing the key turn in the lock. Then there was the mega shock of seeing Flo sitting there as if nothing had happened.

She was in her stripy yellow and pink Babygro, ready for bed, reaching out towards Dad for him to pick her up.

He grabbed her, cuddled her and carried her into the living room before Sharon came downstairs.

I stopped breathing again. One look at my stepmum told me it wasn't over yet – her eyes were red from crying, her whole face was blotchy and she looked like she might blub again at any second.

She stared at me and shook her head. Then she went up to Dad, took Flo away from him and handed her to Zadie. 'Did you find Rochelle?' she whispered.

When he said no, the tears spouted.

'C'mon,' Zadie told me, dragging me out of the room. 'Let's leave them to talk.'

I don't think I started breathing again for a whole half-hour.

Zadie, Flo and I sat in the kitchen listening. Would Sharon turn hysterical? Would she start throwing things and blaming me all over again?

We could hear low voices. Dad was doing a lot of the talking.

'That's a good sign,' Zadie assured me.

Flo fell asleep against Zadie's shoulder. I put the kettle on and made two mugs of tea.

'Yeah, take it through to them,' Zadie nodded, coming down from putting Flo to bed.

I carried the mugs into the hallway, where I could hear what was being said.

'There's no need for us to argue,' Dad was pleading. He sounded really tired. 'Honest, Shaz, I know I haven't been much help lately. I'm the type that buries my head in the sand to avoid trouble. Most blokes are.'

'I've been worried sick about Rochelle,' Sharon confessed between sobs. 'School's been on at me because she won't do any work, and every time I go up to her room, I find her in floods of tears.'

I paused in the hall. Rock-hard Rochelle in floods of tears? That was a new one.

'It's her age,' Dad went on gently. Like, suddenly he knew everything about fifteen-year-old girls. 'You have to expect that kind of thing.'

'And now she's gone missing!' Sharon began to cry again. 'Oh, Tony, what're we going to do?'

I hovered with the tea. Maybe it wasn't a good idea.

'Come here,' Dad said, then Sharon's sobbing grew muffled.

Nope, I could cope, just about, with being shouted at and blamed, but I couldn't walk in on the lovey-dovey stuff. I went back to the kitchen. 'They've made up,' I told Zadie flatly.

Thirty seconds later, Dad and Sharon followed me. He had his arm around her shoulder, she was holding a soggy tissue. She came up to me and took my hand.

I was still expecting *You stupid kid!* and *It's all your fault!* The same old stuff.

'Marsha, I'm sorry you didn't win the Face of the Year,' she said.

Fifteen

How deep did that sorry go? You'll be wondering this, and so am I.

Anyway. Dad and Shaz are staying together, for better or worse.

After Sharon had apologized to me, she and Dad made a million phone calls.

'Have you seen Rochelle?' they asked every single friend and enemy she had, plus the woman who owned the flower shop, plus the taxi drivers at the rank outside the station.

Negative. Blank. Zilch information. We didn't even know if Rochelle had got off the train. By now it was dark, and more than twenty-four hours since she was last seen.

'We have to call the police!' Sharon decided. She crumbled as she spoke the words, as if the game was moving to the next level – uniforms, search parties, appeals on the radio and TV.

'She can look after herself, don't worry,' Zadie tried to tell us.

Dad had the deciding vote. 'Let's just try a few more calls. Who haven't we contacted yet?'

Sharon fetched Roche's address book and found some more numbers.

Sorry u didn't win, Stef texted me. **See u 2morrow.**

Rochelle's legged it, I texted back. **Big mystery. Have u seen her?**

I was out in the back garden for some peace and quiet.

When I looked up I thought I'd seen a ghost, but it was only Scott sneaking across the grass.

'God, Marsh, you scared the life out of me!' he yelped.

'Me too.' I'd jumped up and dropped my phone. I hadn't even thought about him in the last forty-eight hours, which is normal because Scott acts like he's completely detached from everything in the world except his precious footie team. He comes and goes, drifts in and out, vanishes without anybody panicking and calling the police. I often notice this difference between the way Sharon treats her son and her daughter, even though Scott's a year younger.

'What're you doing?' I screeched.

'I'm collecting some CDs. I didn't think there was anyone in.'

'If you looked on the drive instead of sneaking round the back, you'd see Dad's car,' I pointed out. 'Plus, your mum and Flo are back as well.'

Scott frowned.

'Yeah, they're not getting divorced,' I acknowledged. 'Aren't you glad? And your mum said sorry to me.'

'For what?'

I stretched the truth a bit. 'For letting Roche be mean to me.'

'Whoa!' he said, backing off. 'Don't drag me into that stuff!'

'I'm not dragging you in, I'm only telling you. Scott, where are you going? I thought you wanted your CDs.'

As soon as I'd mentioned Rochelle, he'd turned around. 'Forget it,' he muttered.

'Listen, Scott, Roche has done a runner. You haven't seen her, have you?'

He was gone without answering, even though I was sure he'd heard. He must've practically bumped into Jude, who dumped his bike at the back gate and came charging up the path.

'It's true then?' Jude asked, looking like he'd mountain biked up and down a whole mountain to get here. 'Rochelle's vanished?'

At the sound of his voice, Zadie came dashing outside. 'Jude!' she cried, flinging herself at him. 'You got my message?'

More lovey-dovey stuff made me back off into the house.

'OK, call the police,' Dad was saying to Sharon. 'We can't go another whole night without informing them.'

The weird thing was, his decision made Sharon pull herself together at long last. She was the one who dialled 999 and calmly explained the problem. She didn't hesitate as she gave them details about Rochelle's last known movements and a brilliant description, down to the colour of her socks. Work that one out.

'Dad, where's Scott staying?' I asked quietly while Sharon spoke to the police. I couldn't get over how weirdly my stepbrother had acted, even for him.

'At a mate's,' Dad shrugged, trying to listen to Sharon.

'Yes, but which one?'

He frowned. 'A kid with an unusual name – foreign sounding.'

Sharon put the phone down, her face pale and puffy. 'They're sending someone round,' she told us.

'Shaz, where's Scott?' Dad asked, to distract her.

She shook her head and sighed. *Don't bother me.* Then she seemed to change her mind. 'Yes, perhaps we'd better let him know what's happened. After all, he's part of the family.'

Really? You could've fooled me.

'Where is he?' I nagged. 'I'll go and fetch him.'

'He's at Enrique Stewart's,' she frowned. 'Just down the end of the street.'

Sharon didn't have to tell me where Enrique lived. If you like someone as much as I like him, you collect every scrap of information, like where they went for their last haircut and how often they clip their toenails.

Enrique's birthday is on March 28th, Aries. He's fifteen, even though he's in Scott's year because he didn't speak English when he first came to the school so they kept him down a year. He lives at 63 Wentworth Road.

I was down that road faster than you can say Man United.

'Is Scott here? I need to talk to him,' I jabbered at Enrique when he answered the door. This was only the third time I'd ever spoken to him, even though I'd adored him for six whole months.

'Don't let her in!' Scott yelled from the top of the stairs, making a cross with his forefingers like I was the Devil.

'Yes, he's here,' Enrique had to admit. 'What's up with that?'

'Nothing. I need to see him. Rochelle's gone missing. They're calling the police.'

Enrique stared at me with his big brown eyes.

'Scott, don't you care about your sister?' I yelled. 'This is serious. She got on a train in London yesterday evening, and no one's seen her since!'

His friend turned around and took the stairs two at a time. 'Call yourself a mate!' he muttered, flinging open a bedroom door and promptly dragging Rochelle out.

Between them, Scott and Rochelle had conned Enrique into letting her stay at his place. His mum and dad were away for a few days, so there was plenty of room.

Only, they'd omitted to tell him that she

was in deep trouble with me, Zadie, Domenico Lane, Stacey Nicholls and just about everyone in the entire universe.

'Sure you can stay,' Enrique had said, believing her story about losing her door key and everyone in our house being away for the weekend. She'd kipped in the bed belonging to a sister who was away at college.

Scott, though, knew she was on the run and thought it would be cool to play along for a while.

'Scott, how could you?' Sharon demanded later.

He shrugged and yawned, switched on the telly.

As far as I'm concerned, Scott is a total lost cause.

The first Enrique knew there was anything wrong was when I came knocking at the door.

You've never seen kids vanish so quick as Scott and Enrique did when Rochelle and I came face to face. If there's one thing boys are good at, it's not sticking around when girls are about to have a fight.

'What do you want, Marsha?' Rochelle demanded, stalking along the landing and down the stairs.

I stared up at her.

She joined me in Enrique's hallway, beside the full-length mirror. And there we were, the two of us, captured in that tall oblong of silvery glass.

Me with my too-big mouth and stroppy expression, her with her blonde streaks and make-up.

I tried my hardest to remember what Zadie and Sharon had said about Roche being jealous and the reasons why she'd tried to ruin my life. I made myself flap my wings and float above all the hard feelings.

'Dad and Sharon have made up,' I told her. 'She's brought Flo back home.'

Home. One family. United.

Then Roche broke down and cried.

'Aren't you glad?' I asked, doing my parrot, repeating thing. It was a shock to me to see her blubbing.

'God, I wish they'd make up their minds!' she sniffed.

'They're there now,' I convinced her. 'They've talked the whole thing through.'

'Until the next time.' *Deep breath*.

'Aren't you coming?'

'In a minute.' *Sniff, sniff*.

'They've called the police.' I had to say this bit straight out, without softening it to save her feelings. We had to get a move on before the sirens came waah-waahing down the street.

She jumped a mile. 'What for? Are they gonna arrest me?'

'No, stupid. You only told a lie and they don't put you in prison for that. They're setting up a search party because you went missing. Only now they don't have to, do they?'

I wouldn't say that Rochelle was grateful exactly.

grateful *adjective*
1. feeling or expressing thanks: 'I'm *grateful* for the help you gave'

2. welcome or acceptable: 'a *grateful* breeze cooled their brows'

Word family: **gratefully** *adverb,* **gratefulness** *noun*

She never said thanks. But she did promise she would try not to be mean to me in future.

I can see you thinking that leopards don't change their spots.

In other words, trying not to be jealous is like going on a diet – you tell yourself not to eat doughnuts, but it's not that easy when one's sitting on the plate in front of you oozing jam and cream.

Sometimes I catch Roche staring hard at me, and I know what that's about.

Like now, while Zadie is pointing her Fuji Finepix at me.

'Look over your shoulder, head down, straight at the camera – cool!' *Click.* 'Again, Marsh. Bring your left arm up on to your hip, put your shoulders back!' *Click, click.*

Melanie Duchamp has told Rochelle that

she doesn't want her on her 13–17 list after all, but she's booked me for a fashion shoot with a big pre-teen mag. Meanwhile Zadie's building up my portfolio.

Poor Rochelle – and I mean it.

I'll tell you something before I go. Somehow Roche managed to blag her way into Enrique's good books. She said all the sorries and thank yous she didn't say to me to him instead. *Sorry I dropped you in it, thank you for not being mad with me!*

Enrique fell for it. He asked her out on a date and now they're an item.

Try to imagine how I feel about that.

Stef, Lisa and I bumped into them holding hands in D corridor earlier today.

'Look a bit more cheerful, for heaven's sake!' Zadie tells me, flashing an opal ring that Jude bought her.

('It's so *not* an engagement ring!' she tells everyone.)

I smile at the camera.

Sharon and Dad are still together, Zadie's secretly engaged to her childhood sweetheart, Roche is going out with Enrique

Stewart (boo-hoo), and I, believe it or not, am fairest of them all.

Yeah, it's bizarre how things work out.

bizarre (say *biz-ar*). It comes after **biweekly** *adjective* and before **blab** *verb*.

HARMONY HARRIS CUTS LOOSE

by Jenny Oldfield

Who'd have thought my life would turn into a fairy tale? Not me for a start. But then I never believed in the wicked stepmother, fairy godmother stuff either. And, wow, was I wrong!

So my mum gets ill and I have to stay with my mega-rich aunt and uncle. Nightmare! Meet lovely Aunt Lucy, who sees me as the poor relation from hell. Meet my delightful cousins, the Brain, the Brat, the Blub and the Blob.

Who needs a handsome prince? Personally, I'd settle for a ticket on the next pumpkin out of here!

THE *DREAMSEEKER* TRILOGY:

Silver Cloud
Iron Eyes
Bad Heart

If you've enjoyed reading about Marsha Martinez, look out for the *Dreamseeker* trilogy, also by Jenny Oldfield.

Winter is in the air and thirteen-year-old Four Winds' small band of White Water Sioux faces extinction. His grandfather, Chief Red Hawk, is close to death, and enemies hound them on all sides. A lonely vision quest brings help in the shape of the mysterious spirit horse, Silver Cloud – but at a cost. Four Winds must leave his homeland to fulfil three impossible tasks. Only then will his tribe be spared.